THE RISEN SERIES BOOK THREE

REMNANTS

A ZOMBIE APOCALYPSE HORROR STORY

PLEASE, LORD,
DON'T LET MY
DAUGHTER SEE ME
DIE TODAY.

MARIE F CROW

Copyright

Remnants is a work of fiction. All names, characters, locations, and incidents are the products of the author's imagination or are used fictitiously. Any resemblance to actual events, locales, or persons, living or dead, is entirely coincidental.

REMNANTS: A NOVEL
Copyright © 2020 by Marie F. Crow
All rights reserved.

Editing by KP Editing
Cover Design by KP Designs
- www.kpdesignshop.com
Published by Kingston Publishing Company
- www.kingstonpublishing.com

Table of Contents

To the fans who have become friends,
And the friends who have become fans,
To the family that is somewhere in between,
And the husband who has been there through it all.

Thank you,

Sugar and Spice and Everything Dies Twice

Marie F Crow

"There are a thousand reasons why someone would take this way out. I only have one reason to keep going." ~Elizabeth Clark

Chapter 1

Once upon a time, there was a perfect girl, with a perfect life, in a perfect world. Once upon a time, that was me. Now, nothing is perfect and the fairy tales are finally back to the truth of their origins as "warning tales" for children.

I will throw it all away for love; a love that will be the death of me. In fact, if you are reading this, some person that I have yet to meet, I am most likely already dead. The only way a set of eyes other than my own will rest upon these words is if my eyes are closed to never open again. The way the world is headed, I hope they close soon. I hope they close for good and not to just reopen again later in a lighter shade and foreign to those who once knew me.

This isn't just my story that I write. It's all of ours; all of us who are still trying to survive. Those still trying to pick up the very little that is left for us. Those of us just trying to carry on. Even when we feel utterly alone we are all connected. Now, in this no longer perfect world, we are either trying to survive or we are already dead.

If by some slim chance that I am still alive should you read this, I hope I find you. I hope we meet and we can share your stories - not your stories of today, but your stories of yesterdays. I crave to hear your stories of blue skies and laughter. I want to hear a story of another time when our families were whole and our friends were close. A time before those same people became things we had to destroy and fear.

As I write this my daughter, Genny, and I are hiding in our home. The neighborhood has become a dangerous place. Things that shouldn't be possible now surround us. I don't understand any of it. I only pray that we survive each day. I pray that my daughter, who relies on me completely, never has to watch me die.

A noise from the porch steal my attention from my journal is innocent. It's a simple sound of a creaking board that a week ago I would have normally dismissed as settling. Never before would a wooden moan make my heart leap to my throat, but it does now. It leaps and lodges there, stalling in its beating pattern. My chest burns from forgetting to breathe and the heartbeat that refuses to pump.

I close the notebook that I was writing in slowly as if the paper could betray my presence to the phantom sound. The glow from the gas lantern seems too bright. The room seems too silent. Everything is suspended as if it is straining to see if the noise will come again.

Tension is a breathing, living thing. Its coils are as cold as a python's and its grasp is just as firm. Wrapping around you, it will block your breath and suffocate you. You can't move. You can't breathe. You just sit and wait for whatever is to come.

Genny stirs in her sleeping bag beside me with the invisible python in the room caressing her consciousness. Her eyes blink, attempting to shake the thin veil of slumber and reality before saying to me, "What is it?" her voice seems overbearing, with so much strained silence around us.

I shake my head with no real answers to give her. There could be nothing on the porch. It could very well be just the change of temperatures causing the wooden beams to moan or one of the many large rats that have appeared lately. It could be a stray pet looking for solace. It could be anything and that is what worries me.

Placing a finger over my lips, I crawl to the plywood-covered windows. Living on the coast, hurricane supplies are well stocked and stored at houses. I just never imagined having to install the boards on this side of the windows for safety. I left small slips of spaces between the boards when

I placed them. I told Genny it was for sunlight, but it was honestly for what I am doing now.

The first peek is always the hardest. My mind substitutes the truth for imagined visions. I see in my mind the previous things I have seen with added horrors. The gore is darker. The colors are more vivid. The images are always borrowed from the truth and restyled with cruelty. Sometimes, it is not even images at all. It's the flashes of fears like the hand that swipes at you from under the bed or the eye that is staring back at you through a keyhole. It is nothing whole, but just large enough to stroke your senses to panic.

I want the porch to be empty. I pray that it is empty. The lootings have become brutal in the surrounding areas. With just Genny and I here, we would be easy targets. Police have stopped responding to any emergency calls. The media slaughtered them with claims of excessive force when the first victims of the illness were found, so they stopped responding since they were unable to defend themselves from the attacks. If someone, or something, is on the porch then our protection rests completely on me. It's a heavy fact to accept.

Peering through the thin slice of space, I hold my breath to see if I see anything. Nothing moves around me. There is no creaking or moaning with any movements. No shadows that overcast any spot warning of any hidden dangers. I have to chuckle at myself. My paranoia seems to have gotten the best of me again. Turning to Genny, I smile letting her know that I don't see anything. We both shrug nonchalantly but inside we are rejoicing.

I am halfway back to my previous spot on the living room floor when the sound comes again. It is mocking me. It pokes me with a stick dipped in dares that asks if I am brave enough to look again. I'm not, but I don't have a choice.

There is nothing nonchalant about my daughter now. She is sitting up, her body wrapped with the same python I thought I had chased away. It is back and it is squeezing us even harder this time.

The moaning of the creaking sound becomes a pattern. It is a long drawn out high pitch sound before being followed by a quicker, shorter imitation. I know what and who it is.

"It's okay." I smile at Genny and try to convey the statement with my face. It might be okay, but what would cause my neighbor to be hiding on my porch at this hour? My mind draws blank, but I keep my face hopeful and tell her, "It's just Mr. Allen. I'll go see what he wants."

She nods her head with her eyes missing the conviction of my words. "Be careful," she whispers to me. "He could be sick."

I want to reassure her with feelings that I don't possess. I tell her, "He is probably just checking on us. Doing his nightly rounds."

She nods her head again, but she doesn't buy the pep talk.

The deadbolt is as loud as a rifle firing into the night. I cringe, a little startled by the unexpected level of it. Mr. Allen, the forced retired town sheriff, sits in a white rocking chair on my porch. The chairs are just out of sight of the peephole which is why I didn't see him when I first looked. He is dressed in his normal blue jeans and white cotton tee-shirt that I have become accustomed to seeing him wear. The salt and pepper coloring of his hair catches the moonlight as he passes in and out of the shadows with his rocking motion.

He may have given up the uniform, but he can't shake the years of shouldered responsibilities he once had. Instead of watching over the town, he now watches over our neighborhood and we are all grateful. We have been assured that this will all pass, but until then he has sworn to do his best to keep us all safe.

With that in mind, it is not uncommon to find him on my porch at odd hours. My house is the last of his patrol and the rockers call to him he once said. It is my hope that his added presence only helps to sway any vandals not to pick my house. Normally though, he does knock first.

"Hey Allen," I called to him, "how did the patrol go?"

He doesn't answer me. He is staring out into the street as if his mind is a thousand miles away. He continues to rock, a steady motion of the back and forth of the chair in the shadowed corner of the porch with the wood mocking the motion.

"Allen?" I call again. My voice is unsteady from the unnatural behavior from the man who I know as a friend

Allen is normally upbeat and cheerful, if not a borderline smartass. When many officers of the law become jaded with the abuse from the public, Allen found it amusing. He tells stories of his days with a smile and laugh about indignant speeders or the erratic drunks before finally revealing what over-glorified town member it was. With small town living, there are plenty of over-glorified townsfolk to go around.

"Hey, Allen…" I close the door hoping the wooden barrier will protect Genny. My nerves are jostled with his silence and I have no doubt that she is already watching from the window.

He says something but his voice is so soft that I am unsure if he even spoke. "I killed them," he says a little louder this time.

"What are you talking about?" My voice matches his pitch and our whispered conversation continues.

"All five. I killed all five. Vivie was still in her plaid school uniform," Allen continues to talk, but I don't know this man in front of me. I don't know this empty shell sitting on my porch. His face is blank and grief-filled at the same time.

"I knocked like always," his foreign voice tells me. "When they didn't answer, I was worried about the stuff going on these days. I opened the door. I announced myself before I went in. I didn't want to scare them if it was just a case of everyone being in bed. I called out a few more times standing in that fancy sitting room of theirs. No one answered. It was like the whole house was just empty."

"But it wasn't," I offered for him.

He nods, cementing the information we both know. "But it wasn't."

I sigh, remembering well that "fancy sitting room" of theirs. The Jardens are – were - one of the most lavish families in our neighborhood. They were what we all wanted to be. They had bought a modest home and styled it well; very well. Their five-year-old daughter, Vivie, was just as perfect with bouncing curls to match. Their two boys were spoiled brats, but Vivie made up for the headaches the boys caused.

"They came down the stairs one-by-one and you could tell something just wasn't right. They were looking right at me, but it wasn't right. What Vivie was dragging behind her though, that wasn't right at all." Allen hasn't looked to me this whole speech, but he does now. He looks right at me and his eyes shine with the fear his voice is masking. "She had that damn cat by the tail, but there was no longer any cat. All she had in that small hand was its bleeding tail that she dragged down the stairs behind her. It bounced on every step she took."

The picture he paints for my mind drops my jaw. "They were sick?"

He turns his head away from me again with my question. He nods as he takes a ragged, deep breath before continuing. "I've seen the news; just like you have. You've seen what they can do when sick like that. I told them to stop. I told them, Beth. They just kept coming. I shot the Jardens with Vivie still in that damn school uniform. Still in that damn Catholic school uniform."

The night is silent. Even the bugs have hushed their songs to listen or to hide with shame. There is nothing that I can say to him to help with his grief. I have nothing to encase the emotions that I'm feeling. I look to where I know Genny is sitting and listening to us. I know my daughter is feeling the same grief that we are.

"I did what I had to." I look at him when I hear his voice again. He says, "I had to." He is no longer talking to me now. He is trying to fight the demons inside him that stalk him over his actions "…but it still wasn't right. It still wasn't right, Beth."

I missed the main thread of this conversation when it started. I thought he was here to share his horror, but he is here to confess his sins. I never saw the gun until he placed it in his mouth. His head exploded with the sound of the shot. The roof of his skull completely disappeared in a spray of blood and thicker things against my wall. The sound echoed around me but I can't make a sound as I watch the speckled spots that become long red lines running down the wall behind him.

My mouth hangs wide with the empty choking of my shock, but the night is not quiet. Genny is screaming. She screams with each breath that fuels her terror. She screams as Allen's body still rocks in the chair, a slow pendulum of a headless nightmare.

Chapter 2

When we think of the end of the world most picture flames, giant earth-shattering meteors, nuclear wars, the crash of the stock market, or even Mother Nature with her finest fury that is always displayed on sci-fi shows. At least I did. I never imagined the world that we knew would be destroyed with the very thing we were using to protect ourselves. Vaccines.

There were no alarm bells that first morning sounding its ominous chimes. No loud siren of doom went off to instill fear and panic with its wails. The radio's "system broadcast" came too late, and held no helpful advice to calm our nerves once it did come. The end of the world had snuck up on us and it lept from dark corners, taking most of us with it in those few early days.

News anchors told tales that blended with facts that common sense disputed. It raised eyebrows and jokes over grainy news footage pictures they showed. In fact, no one took any of it seriously until it was too late. The jokes became no longer funny when the news footage was of someone you knew. Eyebrows rose over shock and not amusement when it was happening at our feet and no longer on the televisions. Fear was becoming a fact of life and then, there were no more news anchors or radio broadcasts. It was silence in static form.

Social media became the fastest way to keep up with what was happening around the world, but even then, we still couldn't fully believe the posted pictures.

We are a proud species, believing that we are safe and untouchable. "Nothing like that could happen to me. That only happens to other people." That is what we tell ourselves. On that morning, everyone was touched and no one was safe. When social media stopped, we became isolated, discovering information only from the stories told by those left around us. Stories that we were forced to suddenly very much believe.

I had kept Genny home from school that day. There was no foretelling with a misty dream or a "feeling in my gut." I was just not a fan of a forced vaccine. A vaccine I would have most likely taken her for anyway on my own dime. It was the principle of the matter. It should be up to me, the parent, what shots my child receives and not the government "for the better of the people." What a twisted joke that turned out to be. I am also a pro-pouter when told I have to do something that I don't want to do. Just ask my ex.

Charlie and I have been divorced for years. Since then, it has been just Genny and myself relearning the term "family" and all that it can hold for us. So, when the dawn came that morning, there was no one for me to hide behind or to look to for help. There was no male to send down into alleyways first or any strong arms to cry into while they held me. It was all up to me to keep us safe.

s parents, we always joke that kids don't come with handbooks telling us what to do. We have to figure it out on our own. Doomsday didn't come with a handbook either. Just like being a parent, I am still trying to figure it out on my own.

That is why we, Genny and myself, are now living in a crypt in the graveyard on the outskirts of town. There are no neighbors to give away our location. There is no one to knock in the middle of the night asking to borrow items such as ammo, guns, or food. The dead are quiet and it is almost peaceful to look out during the day and see the rolling hills with the many statues and the crosses that lean from the many years of neglect. Sometimes I can almost forget what we are living through. Sometimes.

There is no foot traffic here. It helps to keep whatever those things are which now hunts us like animals, as we once hunted so many other animals, away from this area. I guess people don't come to see the dead when there are so many dying every day all around us.

The crypts are set far enough back that even if there was a road driving through, we would be safe from sight. The thick stone walls hide our scent, making these new predators miss our presence. The few that have come by, for whatever reason, without any windows to peer into to see us have never hesitated outside. As far as other people, the cemetery holds no supplies, making it barren of panic-driven looters. It is just Genny and I in this small private crypt and the many true dead that lay in coffins around us and under us. I don't mind these dead, no matter what the extra nails in their coffins may imply

"Why do you always write in that thing?" Genny's annoyed voice signals that the nightly, "I'm bored" routine is about to start.

"Why do you always ask me obvious questions?" I close the newest addition to the growing catalog of notebooks as journals that I keep. At first, I looted them as needed for kindling for fires and the many other life's necessities that the proper paper items are becoming in short supply. Over time however, they became an escape. A place to jot down what stores were already empty, what places were overrun and where the most unsavory have claimed as their own. I used them to make lists to keep my mind focused when the panic struggled to take over. I used them to make plans should we become in danger. Now, I just use them to unburden the thoughts that I can't share with Genny.

"Um, because there is no one else to talk to around here?" Genny's comment holds more meaning for me than it does for her.

This is not how a sixteen-year-old should be living. Her long brown hair is held high in a throw together of a thick bun style. Strands of hair have escaped, framing her face and long neck. They hang limp without their normal shine and bounce from the recent lack of washing to which her hair was accustomed. Her clothes, a possession that once defined her and her friends, show the abuse of constant wearing with faded colors and shredding.

Friends that she used to spend hours with on the phone texting and calling, making me dread each phone bill, are no longer surrounding her with conversations and laughter. I know sometimes when her mind wanders, she is wondering if they are held up somewhere like this, unsure of what the future brings, too. This is not the life I had planned for her, and as her mother, I can't help but feel guilty over her misery.

"That is not true. Mr. Welton over there looks bored to death. I'm sure he would love to hear your positive outlook on life." My horrible humor is met with an eye roll that would strike a lesser person with shame. As a mother though, I am immune to eye rolls, stomping of feet and slamming of doors.

"I can always call Ginjer over?" It is more of a threat than a question and it has its desired results.

"So, tell me, Mr. Welton, how do you enjoy your darker mahogany over the plain light pine of your relative here?" Genny drops her voice to a mockery of a serious debate, her face matching the false, dedicated tone. She nods and responds with a deep fascination to the pretend conversation and I smile. Her mood swings can bring me to fits of frustration, but at least she can still find the humor of this life.

I should feel ashamed of using Ginjer as a joke to avoid dealing with a teen's mood swing, but I have done much greater sins to preserve my survival and sanity than ridiculing my past employer. I used to clean houses to help the days between paychecks seem less bare with the constant demands of supporting a "me generation" youth. This need is how I met the woman who filled my weekends with hidden laughter over her comments about life. Ginjer, with a "J," as she would always introduce herself as if that made it sound more exotic and herself more important. Neither of which are true.

Ginjer was one of my main "clients." Her home was always spotless, but it looked better for the neighbors to see a service, as she called me, to come once a week. I was never really there to clean because everything already had its perfect place. I do believe she would measure the spacing between items after I left just to be sure nothing was ever amiss. I was there to fill the long hours of privileged, housewife boredom.

The tanned and toned Goddess did not have children to run amok, smearing prints along polished surfaces. Just a designer dog with more clothes than Genny and I owned put together and a husband who traveled a lot, allowing way too much alone time for Ginjer. I often wondered if that was why the screws were so loose with her thinking or if the privileged really just have a different set of mental tools from which to work. A set of much duller tools.

After Allen killed himself on my porch, the images of the many bloody survivors filling the hospital beds with wide eyes and torn limbs began showing up on the televisions. With its tall, scrolling, metal-gated driveway and various vacant rooms, her house seemed like the perfect place to stay until we could figure out what was really going on. When she met us at the gate wearing garlic bulbs like strands of pearls, a spray bottle of Holy Water and had us "help" her remember the Lord's prayer to be sure we were who we claimed to be, I had started to rethink the idea. I do have to commend the woman for having every legend of lore antidote memorized, though. If she had had silver bullets, she may have shot us.

Despite Ginjer's wrath, the three of us and her dog, Mintzy, not willing to risk our lives for the no longer valuables inside the house, left once the looting started. She stays five "houses" down now in a more established crypt and yes, as if anyone should ever come visit, the original occupants are all perfectly arranged.

"The nights are getting colder." My voice breaks into the one-sided exchange Genny was holding. "Think any of them are wearing jackets?"

"Mom, that is disgusting! They are wearing them!" Even trained to keep our voices at a lowered hush, she can still reach the octaves of perfect teen disapproval.

"Correct. They are wearing them, but not using them. We can do both." I have already been eying the different wooden caskets in their stone archways of rooms for which one looks the most recent, providing the best clothing durability.

"I am really not okay with this. Can you at least wait until morning? When the sun is out?" Genny stands watching me, hugging herself under the few rays of natural light that penetrate the building's roof-top skylight. Her insecurity over the thought of me opening the coffins takes years from her, reminding me of the small girl who once held my hand as we examined the closets for monsters before bedtime.

"Would you feel better about it, then?" I ask her, trying to let her know that what we do now we do because we have to, not because we want to.

"I wouldn't feel worse," she tells me, happy to have avoided doing this under the moon's watch when horrible things feel so much more dangerous.

I nod, agreeing to wait until the sun's warmth can chase away the heebie-jeebies for us both.

"Let's just get some sleep. There is a store that is not crossed off yet that I want to explore tomorrow." I hold my voice to a neutral pitch, refusing to let her gather any hope from my words. I know what this store holds will not bring me the 'thank yous' and hugs that finding the stash of youth-themed magazines had earned me.

Genny offers no come back of exasperated efforts at the thought of having to "raid" tomorrow. It only proves to me how unsettling the idea of clothes hunting from the dead is to her. I wish I had the luxury not to be unsettled by the things I have had to do, but I don't. Luxury was something I never had before and I don't have it now. Now, I have the very real fact of a child I must protect from a world that I do not understand.

We settle into the arched alcove we have claimed as our bedroom. Together, we had cleared out the cobweb-hugged coffins in this space, using them as a barrier between the open archway and us. We truly sleep under the shadow of the dead, hiding from the dead, with our shredded blankets and limp pillows protecting us from the cold cement floor.

he last thought that always escorts me to sleep finds me again with the guilt that it always carries. *This is not the way a sixteen-year-old should be living.*

Chapter 3

There is a noise. A sharp, annoying, persistent noise reaching through the walls of our "home." It reminds me of my neighbor's yapper, and it must mean she has let it out for its morning duty. The alarm clock will be going off soon signaling the start of my day with blaring rudeness. I stretch, keeping my eyes closed, under the thick blanket of my comforter which I refuse to give up no matter the season. Some things just should not be left up to debate for a groundhog.

Something feels wrong, though. There are no more alarm clocks. The bed barely holds any warmth and the mattress is firmer than I remember. My comforter that was my snuggle buddy, has lost a lot of its weight, making it thin and depressing. The room seems darker than normal behind my closed eyelids, making me wonder exactly what time it is.

Mitzy and Genny are in bed with me, which seems only to add to my confusion. Confusion lifts from me with the force of slamming into a brick wall when I remember everything. The wall of my panic, sold and forceful, jolts me awake.

"Mom, is that Mintzy?" Genny's voice trembles with fear. The dog only barks at strangers. Someone is in the cemetery with us. At least, I hope it is a "someone."

If I open our door, it will give away our hiding spot to whoever, or whatever, is out there. If I don't open our door, and Ginjer is in trouble, I can't help her. The very fact of no windows to keep us safe is now keeping us blind.

Do I risk the safety of my daughter for the benefit of a friend? If I don't, and something does happen to Ginjer, will I be able to live with it? If I do, and something happens to Genny, will I be able to live with that?

"What are you doing?" My mind is racing with imagined events and Genny's panic-filled hissing does not help to settle the images.

"I can't open the door. They will find us if I go out there. They may find you." Even to myself, my words sound like a coward.

"You don't even know if someone *is* out there. Mintzy could just be barking because Mrs. Ginjer is hurt." Her voice rises in octaves with each word. She is ashamed of me, but if it keeps her safe, I can live with it.

"The only time that dog barks is if someone comes around it doesn't know. The damn thing just sat there when Ginjer laid on the floor for three hours after falling down the stairs trying to figure out which heels to wear to a party. Someone *is* out there." I try to fill my voice with anger to back her arguments down, but I recognize that fire in her eyes. After all, she got it from me.

"If you do not go out there, I will." Genny's steady voice matches the look in her eyes.

If it were anyone else, I would call their bluff, but it is not. It is Genny. I once admired her backbone and bravery, but right now, I find it rather mistimed and misguided.

"I'll go, but you stay," I tell her, because caving to her demands seems easier than sitting on her to keep her safe.

"No, I'm going, too." Her desire to join me is more from her fear of being left here alone than her need to save anyone. That fire of a fighter that was in her eyes is now flickering with uncertainty and losing its glow.

"That is not the deal. I go. You stay. Or, we both stay. You choose." Leaving the option of life or death in the hands of a teenager may not seem fair, but nothing is really fair anymore. If Genny is to survive now, she has to start thinking for herself. Truth is I may not always be around to help her or counsel her decisions.

"I'll stay." It is a whisper of consent.

"If I don't make it back," my words cause her jaw to drop with shock, "listen, if I don't make it back, take the green notebook for a list of stores that we have not yet checked. The purple notebook has escape plans for getting out of the city without being seen. Avoid the main roads. You need to remember this, Genny. Can you do that?"

"I won't need to. You'll come back, Mom. It may just be a raccoon or something and here you are going all doomsday on me." Genny hugs herself, trying to convince herself of her words as much as she is me.

"Huney, I went "all doomsday" months ago, but I really do hope it is just a raccoon." I place a kiss on the top of her forehead and grab the last flashlight left to us. If I am going out to meet my death, I want to see it coming.

With hinges that no longer fully support the weight, the stone door grates along its porch when I swing it open. The sound seems to be louder than I remember. It shouts without words into the night *Look, we have another one over here* for all to hear. Mintzy's barking is rapid and clipped. It echoes in the night air giving it the illusion that it never ends.

From where I stand, peering through the sliver of a crack of our door, I can see down the row of many family crypts. The moon is high but not full, providing the shadows with the ability to grow tall and menacing. There is nothing that quite inspires bravery in a person like the dark, thick shadows of a graveyard.

Refusing to turn my back on the shrouded darkness, I close the stone door of my new home with my back, filling my head with the pleadings for it only to be a raccoon. I used to think I was brave. I would creep down hallways with a wooden baseball bat raised high overhead, investigating odd sounds in the night in our house. I would walk with my head high and the metal keys of my car wedged between the fingers of my fist through dark parking lots after long hours at work. As I stand here, shaking to my core, I know that anything I may have encountered then has no comparison to the monsters I may meet now.

My tennis shoes seem to have developed an amazing skill of finding every limb or dry leaf. They send the sounds of their betrayal into the air. My feet seem to stumble over raised roots or uneven cement edges that I have never noticed until now. It would be almost comedic if it were another, not myself, creeping through the tall stone crypts searching for what is going bump in the night. Being as it is me, I don't find any of it funny. What I find when I finally reach Ginjer's "home" is even less of a gag reel and of course, it is not a raccoon.

"Why can't it ever be a raccoon?" I ask myself from my shadowed shelter.

There are three of them illuminated in the dark by the provided moonlight. They are standing still with only their heads moving and I know from watching these monsters work that they are trying to find a way inside. They are not mindlessly beating on the door like you would expect from monsters. They do not moan or make unnecessary noises giving clues to their next move or nature. They are more frightening to watch than any movie screen has ever provided, because they are plotting, thinking and waiting for the answers to come to them. Answers that always do.

heir clothing still looks new, missing the signs of numerous attacks upon others. I hope this means that they are not as adept at death as some of the others have been. A skill they seem to pick up on well by stalking us as they now try to watch Mintzy through the stone walls with their dedicated stares. Their heads follow the barking dog as it runs up and down the wall from the inside and I wonder why Ginjer has done nothing to silence him. As their heads turn to me following the dog's path, I realize my mistake at being lost in thoughts for another when my own life is at risk.

I know the moment they become aware of me with their eyes sliding along the stone pathway to me. I know because one of them growls from the depths of his throat. He seems to smile at me and my spine goes to water with the sight. We are in a stand-off, each waiting to see what the other will do now that they have discovered me. Their bodies are held stiff and rigid, ready for the attack if I should attempt to run. Their eyes survey me, looking for a weakness and a threat that may harm them. I hold none and they know it. Their resolve for victory makes my heart thud so loudly I am sure they can hear it.

If I turn to run, I will lead them back to Genny. That is not a risk that I am willing to take, but I know I will not survive if I attempt to fight them in the open like this. I have seen what they have done to grown men twice my size with no effort. They are stronger than I am. I am alone, making me that much more vulnerable, but they don't have a child to protect like I do. That fact alone is what provides me with the need to live each day. It provides me with the strength to keep fighting for each day.

I know that if I don't run, they won't run. They prefer to stalk their prey, drawing out the death either for their pleasure or with hopes to tire us out, making us easier to kill. They have all the patience, because they have all the time. They do not become scared, or frightened of things that may happen resulting in plans destroyed by panic. They keep their emotions in check until the last moment, right before they attack. That last moment that is always our death and their delight.

I need a plan and I need one now. They are already figuring out how to take me down and are spreading out to surround me. They will not rush me like a pack of wild dogs. They communicate somehow, silently, bringing down their prey with group precision. I have become the center of focus for this group and with each of their steps forward, I feel one of mine backwards.

My feet stumble where theirs glide. My body grows sweaty with panic while they stay calm. My mind is racing as I look for anything, I may use against them, or for a way out, I find nothing and then it finally happens. I trigger their attack.

Tripping over a hidden step that lies in deep shadows, I feel my body tumble backwards. Lightning flashes in my mind when my head bounces off the cement, blinding me with pain. I sense their shadows over me, jolting me conscious for the attack. The first male launches his body over mine, almost like a shield from the others, but it is not chivalry. He just wants the first bite.

His hot breath rolls over my face, turning my head from the weight of its rankness. His skin is perfect, unmarred by death and such a contrast to how monsters appear in fiction. His desires match those monsters perfectly though with his jaw wide and eyes blaring with hate. There is no confusing what he is as he struggles against me.

My extended arms brace the flashlight between my hands, using its metal as a guard against his mouth. His hands tear into my clothing, trying to pull me to him. With thin ribbons of pain, I can feel his nails discovering my flesh. The smell of my blood will cause them to fight harder amongst themselves for me; for any small morsel of my warm flesh that they can scrape free. I am running out of time. I need that plan, now.

His body is keeping the other two from really reaching me with a dog-pile effect. My arms begin to shake with the strain of supporting their weight. As his wet saliva begins to flow around the flashlight, dripping onto my face, only one escape comes to mind. I finally realize that the only weapon I have available to me, is me.

I pull down against the flashlight, extending his jaw wider, and take a deep breath. Blocking all thoughts of doubt from my mind, I force my forehead into his upper face with repeated blows. His nose breaks, coating me with his blood and spraying it along the cement floor of the crypt's porch. It runs down my face in paste like gore, sticking to me before sliding down my neck. It is warm and slippery, slithering along my flesh and I fight against my stomach's rebellion.

So unprepared for a return attack, and the damage it does, my assault stuns him. His eyes blink rapidly in confusion and his body goes stiff with his thoughts. I was hoping for this moment. With his fingers now untangled from my shirt, I can twist, throwing the dog-pile of death off me. They land in an ungraceful heap with their stunned comrade pinning them and I run. Their howls of anger follow me into the darkness, giving speed to my legs, because I know they will be right behind me. You can't hide from death, but you can run.

I am spitting out black clumps of blood and thicker things that trail from my forehead into my mouth. My head aches from colliding with the bones of his face. The cold night steals the air from my lungs in a reverse style of CPR. I can feel my sides cramping like blades stabbing into my chest. The overexertion of my body causes me to be clumsy and I fall to the ground with a crawl. I can hear them behind me and I take cover under the shadows of the folded wings of an angel.

Haloed by the many sparkling stars in the night's sky, her blank stone eyes stare down at me with sadness. Her hands seem to reach for me with long graceful fingers, offering help that I know she can't provide. Her faded white gown flows around her legs with many folds, frozen in a false wind. She has mourned for whoever is buried here for years. Now, as she stares at me with white, wide eyes, she mourns for me.

The pause of the brittle sound effects from the many fallen leaves tells me the monsters' steps have slowed as they seek me. I can picture their eyes searching the shadows for me as my scent mingles with the blood from the broken nose, giving them hints of my location. My shirt is starting to stick to my stomach and I know that it will not be just his blood that will tell them where I am.

Scuffed leather loafers step beside me. They are inches from my legs as he tries to find what his nose is telling him is near. Any air that I have recovered escapes with panic, pulling short gasps from my lungs. He will turn soon and find me here, hunched like a small child afraid of what hides in the night. There is no more running. The moon slips behind grey clouds with its cowardice, and the angel closes her eyes with the resulting shadows.

My eyes are so glued to the loafers beside me, that I never hear the monster sneaking up behind me. A firm hand snatches me by my ponytail and drags me with brutal speed backwards across the grave plot. The female pulls me directly under her face, peering down at me, turning from side to side as if trying to choose the first spot of my flesh to attack. Her long red hair, styled in the same fashion as mine, coils around her neck like a serpent. Her eyes are a muted green with the artificial life that now stares at me. Her face is pale with blue-black veins streaking across it with a demonic beauty. Her mouth that is slowly stretching wide with her planned attack, is as black as rot with a smell that matches it.

She is pinning me with my hair and shoulders, learning from my attack on her "friend."

She is enjoying watching my face fill with my fears and pets my hair with a bloated finger, further unsettling me. With my eyes unable to move from hers, my hands search blindly in desperation for something to use against her.

My frantic fingertips brush against something cold and solid. It touches them with a silent, voluntary offering of itself. I stretch, extending my fingers to a point that is almost painful, latching onto the object. Swinging with a wide arc, I strike the monster across the side of her face with a heavy glass vase left by past mourners. The dried flowers sail as she tilts sideways, her head swaying with the blow. She loses some of her strength, dazed by the attack, allowing me to sit up. I do not wait for her to collect herself, but swing the vase repeatedly into her face and listen to them both crack with each connection.

Her face becomes a slow ruin with her bones breaking and the pale flesh lacerating. Those black-blue veins seep dark blood that splashes with a fine mist over my face and hands, making the glass slippery. I secure the vase, grasping it around the indented neck where a yellowing white ribbon is tied, and bring it down one final time. The resonating crack of bones leaves her still and the final crack of the glass leaves the vase shattered in my hands. Both lay before me broken, covered in blood and catching the light of the stars in the crimson glow.

I want to relax. My body begs for it with the way fear can steal so much from a person. Still clasped in my hand is a large piece of the neck of the glass vase with only the blood-soaked white ribbon keeping the razor edges of the glass from slicing me. My fingers are locked around it, refusing to release the weapon of my salvation like a memento of a well-won battle. When I see the loafers standing beside me again, I am grateful for the small shard.

His palm wraps around the top of my head, pulling it to the right, exposing the long line of my neck. My spine aches under his strength and it feels as if my muscles will tear from being forced to such a degree of an angle. With one hand, he has immobilized me, unable to stand up or move forward with the weight of his strength and the angle of my torture.

Sobs escape from my throat with the pain he is causing me. Pain is so extreme that I can't think of a way to fight back. The pain causes a haze of flashing agony along my spine that rips into my head, removing any thoughts of fighting. I am ready to cave under the pain, to give myself over to death if it would stop. I would be free from it all. Just as I make my peace with what is about to happen, one word refills my soul with fire.

"Mom!" Genny's scream startles us both.

I can feel his attention pull from me and my attention pulls forward. His mind will begin to attempt to understand the new information, holding me captive here until he puts together the new pieces of the puzzle.

Genny has bought me time, confusing the monster that holds me with her presence, and I don't plan to waste it. My neck is forced to such an angle that his wrist is exposed with his firm grasp on my head. I close my eyes and offer a prayer to the silent angel that has kept watch over this spot for years. *Please Lord, don't let my daughter see me die today.*

The glass bites into my hand with my slicing of his wrist. I can feel it slide across his tendons like the plucking of the strings of a harp. Instantly, thick, clumped liquid rains over my shoulder, soaking my shirt and neck with his sour smelling blood. The strength of his hand is gone with the damage I have caused to his wrist. It frees me from my pain, allowing my mind to focus once again. The glass is three layers thick now with blood and the ribbon can no longer provide me protection from the razor-like edge. The pain from my palm is laced with fire as the glass shreds my hand as it shredded his wrist, but it is the best weapon I have.

This sharp, fragile blade has to find its mark to save us. It has to kill him, or he will keep coming for us. There is only one spot on their body that seems to result in their deaths: the head. I guess, at the height of the male monster and stand, pivoting upwards in a spiral, aiming the glass shard at his temple. The glass slides through his temple like it's made of cardboard while taking its vengeance on my palm. He stumbles, falling to his side, but his eyes still watch me. The shard is not long, or strong, enough to reach the needed goal. It has only slowed him and already he is trying to come for me again.

The world escapes me. The blackness of night shrinks down to the dull, almost gray eyes staring at me. Genny's screams are even slowed. Her syllables seem exaggerated as she pleads with me to run. I can't run. Death will always find you when you run.

With a resolve I would never have guessed I possessed; I stomp against the spot nestling the shard. My tennis shoe drives it further into his skull with each forceful act. All of my fear is gone now. Anger replaces it and I use it to give me strength.

I am angry over being attacked. I am angry over how we must live now. I am angry that every day and night we fear these monsters finding us and what it could mean for us. Hot tears clear their way through the drying blood that cakes my face. My legs are being splashed with blood that is thicker than the many layers of my rage. Only when I have caused enough damage that the fragments of bone and gore rob me of the sight of his eyes, do I stop. I am weak and exhausted, but mostly I'm still just angry.

Chapter 4

The once faded white and serene angel now wears a gown of darker markings. The dark crimson spots are starting to drip down, casting her in a new role. This angel of mourning now walks as an angel of death with the blood and thicker clumps clinging to her hem and feet. A fine mist of red has flowed into the inscription at her feet, highlighting the once hidden words.

Stand not before me and weep. Let not your wails of mourning fill the air around me. For this life's suffering I am free. Soon all will join me and we will rejoice in our victory.

The blood gathers, hovering in the artistic loops of the words before dripping out in small rivers, staining the base. I can't help but to think with envy to myself of how lucky those are who were able to escape before it began.

"I thought I told you to stay inside?" These were not the first words she sought to hear from me and her mood proves that.

"I couldn't just sit in there when I heard you screaming. Sorry." Tears of anger over my attitude and her released fears begin to streak her face.

I don't remember screaming when they first attacked me. Her trembling body shaking with her emotions proves that I must have, though.

I whisper to her with my eyes trying to fight against the many shadows. "We have to get back. There should be one more somewhere."

"I took care of him."

At first, her whispered words do not make sense. She can't possibly mean that she was face-to-face with one of these things. She can't be telling me that she was in danger while I sought to keep her safe. She can't mean that while I was ready to die, she was fighting to survive. Not my precious child.

"He was stunned and stumbling around. He never noticed me. I've seen you take them out before…." Her words trail off, losing their security against my blank glare. Fighting against my feelings, I stare at her with my eyes wide and still like the angel who still looms over us.

"How?" We ask so many questions, that we don't really want to know the answers to in life.

"He was still back along the crypts where some of the markers are just wooden crosses. I used one." She shrugs, as if killing these monsters is just another Monday chore to do before homework.

Giggles bubble forth as I picture my Genny standing behind the male monster with a wooden cross raised high like an overplayed vampire hunter in a novel. I don't mean to mock her bravery or the very real risk she took. Sometimes stress has its own agenda.

Using the only monster hunter I have knowledge of that compares to whatever these things are that hunt us, I ask her, "You staked a zombie?"

"Not exactly," she says, her anger melting to her own giggles with stress relief.

"Buffy has nothing on you, kiddo," I tease her, bringing up her once favorite T.V. show.

"Dunno. I could totally go for an Angel about now." Her smile is enough to make me cringe with the knowledge of her thoughts and I am happy to change the topic.

"Don't get too excited. They are overrated." I leave her confused by my words, as I glance up to the one standing over me still. "Let's go check on Ginjer. Figure out what started all of this."

I walk towards her, holding out one arm in a customary style of embrace. It is her turn to cringe now and she takes a step backwards to avoid the half hug.

"I would totally hug you, but you are gross."

I look down at myself, having forgotten for a moment the war scene of which I wear. My tennis shoes are caked and streaked with an almost clay-like thickness. My jeans are dotted and splashed with dark crimson spots. My shirt is beyond redemption with the many layers and shades of red in an almost tie-dyed swirl of death. It is stained from their blood, but also my own that pulls the cotton material to my stomach. My palm reminds me of the past struggle with the pain that now reawakens. It, too, is covered in layers of blood and staring at my hands covered in such a degree is shocking.

There is never this much detail to deaths in movies. Everything dies quickly. The blood only pools in small, clean circles. There is nothing clean or quick about killing. Blood has no obedience to perfect outlines. It will fill any crevice until it runs too thin, or it is blocked from its path. Hearts fight against death with every beat they can manage. They refuse to stop until they are forced to let go of the desire to live.

"Think she will make me remove my shoes before I enter?" I smile thinking of the woman's distress over the tracks I am sure to make on her perfect floor.

Genny smiles at me with her thoughts of Ginjer's reaction to my appearance. "I think she will make you strip before you enter."

"Well, perhaps I will just give her a big ol' hug with how happy I am she is not hurt." My dare brings real laughter from my daughter. It's a sound that I still cherish, maybe even more now than I did before. "Come on. Let's get this over with."

Our trip back to our "home" is nowhere near as eventful as my trip away. Without the sound of the dog barking, the night is still and silent again. The crackling of our feet treading along the worn pathway across a carpet of leaves gives the only hint to any occupancy. With the danger gone now, the insects of the night slowly begin to sing again.

We come across the last of the monsters, crumpled with a wooden cross pointing skyward from his skull. We don't comment over it or give it much attention. We simply side-step his body blocking our path with mutual understanding that words are not needed.

"You want his jacket?" I smile at her, trying to break the mood.

"You're so twisted." She frowns at me, but I can see her gears turning, debating it.

Watching her weigh the pros and cons of stripping a body that she just had to kill brings a recurring thought to my mind. *This is not how a sixteen-year-old should be living.*

Ginjer's "home" is silent, and after so much noise filling it only moments ago, it adds to my apprehension of what may have happened to her. I would never risk my life by leaving it in her hands, but she is not one normally to hide, either. No, she is much more rehearsed at the "damsel in distress" calling on every avenue of assistance she may need without a moments thought to anyone else's feelings. For her to be hiding now, and not waiting for us with disbelief over how long it took us to save her, does not hold well. I hope it is just an excuse for one of her famous, "no one appreciates me" fits and not something more serious. Bruised egos I am well trained to heal, but bloody, life threatening wounds, not so much.

"Ginjer," I call out as quietly as one can, and still hope to penetrate the stone walls of the crypts. The cemetery may look empty, but I have come not to trust how things appear. My neighbor had looked harmless too, until he began eating his wife. "Ginjer, it's Beth. They are all gone. We are coming in."

I keep my sentences short and soothing in case she is hiding. Mostly because I can't remember if I set the safety on the pistol she has hidden and nothing really says, "thank you," like a near miss with your own loaned gun. The only answer I hear returned is a low growl from behind the door. Good to know Mintzy is still alive. I guess.

Slowly, I pull open the stone door of her ancient crypt. The flames from the many lit candles cause shadows to dance along the walls. They leap and shrink with the breeze from our entrance and the circulation of the air when I close the door. The room is heavy from the different perfumed waxes burning around me and I feel as if I have stepped into a bad vampire movie with so many glowing candelabras. I almost expect one of the coffins to open and a male with a terribly over done widow's peak to sit up, reaching for me with long, pale, boney fingers.

"Ginjer?" My voice echoes in the room, caged by the walls around me. Genny is walking slowly behind me, her nerves fraying with the woman's silence. Only Mintzy's low growl is giving us a hint as to where they may be.

Mintzy is growling from the furthest corner of the crypt. It is closed off in darker shadows with most of the burning candles situated towards the entrance. Ginjer, similar to ourselves, has situated her "room" hidden behind a wall of coffins. The floor is marred with the marks of their movement, giving testimony to the strength one can possess when your safety is the motivation. I pass an alcove once meant to hold urns with its many stone shelves that have been transformed into a closet. Folded piles of pastels are nestled neatly into each pocket of space. The lower area holds shoes of various styles and for a moment, I am almost ashamed of my own "home".

"Is it really you?" A fragmented whisper escapes from the darkness ahead of me.

"Who else would it be?" My relief upon hearing her voice is quickly fading. Perhaps, I am just jealous of her shoes.

"It's us, Mrs. Ginjer," Genny coaxes from behind me. "You can come out now."

"You both could be one of those things!" Sensing its mistress' distress, Mintzy's growl deepens.

"From what I remember, they aren't very chatty," I say, and Genny places her hand on my arm with my frustrations mounting. Genny has the patience of a saint, but for myself I really just want to wash and go back to my not snuggly comforter, not thick mattress and not fluffy pillow that I left to save this woman.

"What is my middle name?"

The woman is serious? Is the first thought that comes to my mind with her demand. It robs me of any politeness I may have been able to grasp.

"The things don't talk. So, they wouldn't know your middle name or even your first name which we have both been calling out like you're a small child and not a grown ass woman. Now get your grown ass out here before I come over there and drag you and your over-bred mutt out here." A part of me may feel guilty for this tone later, but probably not.

My rebuttal is met with the sounds of movement and slowly the Goddess appears. Her strawberry blonde hair is ruffled as if many hands have run through it. Her eye make-up is smeared, spreading the colors wider than she normally applies them. Soft pink lips show signs of chewing with red welts forming in their corners. Even with all of this, she is gorgeous. Sometimes life just isn't fair.

"You don't have to take that vulgar tone with me. You can't blame me for being apprehensive these days!" She adjusts her spoiled pooch under her arm with its blue-bow tied hair. "Why are you so gross? Did you track that in here?"

"Apprehensive, no. I guess you just can't help being-"

"-being careful," Genny talks over my sentence, seeking to ease the foul mood brewing.

"Yes, careful." I force a smile to Genny letting her know that I am on to her. "How did they find you anyway? You being so, careful, and all." My words pause, letting my sarcasm settle in the silence. Sarcasm that is wasted on Ginjer.

"I don't know," is what her mouth says. Her body is very much saying that she knows and it's telling me that we both know I won't like knowing the answer.

"Ginjer, you mean to tell me that after all these weeks of not seeing anyone or any*thing* that suddenly those things find you in the middle of the night and you have no idea why?" My voice holds the annoyance of a parent catching their small child in a lie. Sadly, it has the same effect.

"It wasn't my fault. Well, not exactly. I was walking Mintzy and they saw us."

From years of being a parent, I know that the high pitch of Ginjer's voice means there is still more she is not telling me. A few years, and the gray hairs, from having a teen lets me know that if I just stand here staring at her, she will confess the rest just to have me look away.

"I may have been walking him on the main road, but you're still totally gross!" She shouts the last accusation in a rapid conclusion, hoping her insult will distract me from her confession.

I don't know if I am at a loss for words over how incredibly stupid she is or how incredibly stupid she acts.

"Why? Why would you walk your dog on the road? We have acres of grass around us. Why does he need to be on the road?" I ask her, almost afraid of the answer and how I will handle it.

"The grass stains my heels," she says to me, with complete sincerity. Her mouth forms a small pout with the statement and I know I am going to kill her.

"You risked our safety and your safety over a pair of heels? Do you have any idea how much worse this could have been?" I'm yelling now, and Mintzy squirms in his owner's arms trying to escape my voice.

"But they are-," she begins, but my rage cuts her words short.

"I don't care if they are made by God Himself. If it doesn't protect us, feed us, or shelter us then it is not important! The next time I risk my own neck and the safety of my daughter for you, you better damn well open the door and at least use those damn heels as a weapon." I let my anger flow into each word. The realization that I may have died tonight coming to her aide because she lured those things to us being so stupid sends waves of bitterness through me. Even Genny, the saint, is shaking her head over the gall of this woman.

"Is that why you are so gross?" Ginjer asks me, and it is the last inch of nerve I have to spare.

"No, Ginjer. I am working on my Halloween costume. I am going as Carrie this year." I turn my back to her before my hands find her throat.

"I thought she wore a prom dress?"

Nope, *that* was my last inch.

My feet cannot bring me to the door fast enough. I can feel my tongue mounting an attack and I know once the first shot is fired the battle will stream forth unrelenting. Genny trails behind me, silent and angry with the woman herself. Our backs are a wall of uncaring that glares at her with our retreat.

"Wait," Ginjer calls out carefully. "I don't want to stay alone. Can we stay with you? Just for tonight?"

I want to say no. I want to scream no. All of me does, except for this one small shred of humanity that flickers within as her weakness is so well displayed before me.

I sigh, already regretting the words before I say them. "One night. Tomorrow you have to help us explore a store or you can go hungry." *Perhaps, her heels will feed her.* It is a rude thought, but I smile with it just the same.

"We can do that! Can't we boy?" Ginjer playfully asks the dog, as if it holds an opinion for anything. If he did, he may be more concerned with the bows in his hair.

Genny sighs, sharing a look with me that we have become accustomed to with Ginjer. A look that says we are both baffled by the woman and her actions.

Holding the door open in the fashion that she expects, Genny and I wait as we watch her sway past, exiting before us. We prepare to share another look when her screaming starts. Its high pitch wail sets us to motion, forgetting how very angry we were in the moments past.

This is why they are monsters. Only something spawned from Hell in its most evil of corners could stand before me looking like this. The female that I had beaten with the glass vase stands wrestling Mintzy from the arms of Ginjer. Her fingers are wrapped tightly around the dog's collar, stretching the dog's neck and choking the air from its body. Half of her face is missing from the damage I have caused her. The flesh is jagged, sprinkling blood with each tug that lurches her body. The eye on the side of her face that I attacked hangs loose from its socket, rolling up and down her cheekbone with the motion of a marble on a string. Her lip is torn and it lays flayed, exposing her once white teeth. Her red hair blends into a darker shade with her blood caught in its strands and the sight of her paralyzes me with fear.

"Beth!" Ginjer screams for my help, but all I can do is stand here, blocking Genny and shaking my head with no words forming on my lips. Not even Genny, with her aspirations to save the world, is trying to guilt me into action with condescendingly strained words. She stares with wide eyes as we watch the tug-of-war.

With a sharp popping sound, Mintzy's neck breaks from the strain on his body and his legs go still and limp. Ginjer recoils as if she has been punched, dropping her half of the dog. It is quickly set upon by the female, tearing into fur and flesh with greedy hands. She rakes the meat of the dog into her gaping mouth leaving the blood to pour and pool on the stone porch around her. It steams in the night air, casting an illusion of Mintzy's soul escaping from the tattered form of his body. The three of us are fear-struck, silent and repulsed in a weaving combination of emotions as we watch the female devour the dog with finger sucking satisfaction. With a steady resolve, Ginjer pulls from the waistband of her slacks the pistol I was worried about earlier. The sound of the shot bounces off the surrounding crypts before rippling through the cemetery around us. The female now rests face down into her prize. She is truly dead this time and it's something that I, and nature, had failed to accomplish before. I guess, I forgot to reset the safety after all.

Chapter 5

Ginjer was silent for the rest of the dragging night. She didn't cry over Mintzy or wail with exaggerated memories of the dog. I almost wished she had. The woman was as silent as the fog and just as thick with depression. A voice I have tried to avoid for so many years, I now found myself secretly wishing it would speak if for no other reason than to break the suffocating tension surrounding us.

Genny was also more reserved than normal. I know she was searching her soul for the right words to say to bring comfort to Ginjer. There are no words to encompass the grief that these days keep holding for us. We have suffered deaths by the facts of old age, tragic accidents, or debilitating illnesses before now. Now, death wears the faces of real monsters delivering real horrors. There are no words to take that suffering away.

I dreaded bringing Ginjer along today. The store I have scouted with hopes for supplies I already knew would gain me complaints from Genny. Now, it may be the final buttons for Ginjer's sanity. I don't know if I have the courage to push them. Before Mintzy's death last night, I would have danced across them.

"If you want to stay here, Ginjer," I say, to gain her attention, "we would understand." My voice sounds overly large in the crypt. It is the first voice to echo against these walls since we closed the door last night sealing us in the unspoken depression.

"No. I want to come. I don't want to sit in here. I would have to clean it. I understand it is what it is, but you could at least organize it if you are going to live here."

It is hard to feel sorry for someone that always finds a way to degrade you. Genny beams a huge smile at me with wide eyes trying to remind me of the tragedy that happened last night. My own returned smile is not as polite or as tragic. I'm starting to feel like dancing again.

"If you think that is best." I put a little tune to my voice as I have taught myself with this response to her comments. It is my equivalent of a ,"fuck you, too."

I toss Genny the keys to our Honda so that I may focus on the many empty bags I carry. I hope when we return they will be filled with food. We are running desperately low. Of course, "food" being a very liberal word for what we may find.

Loading the car has become a well-rehearsed chore. Automatically, we scan the area around it, looking for any signs of tampering or loitering. We double-check the seats to be certain it is empty and peer into the space below it also. The image of the hand sneaking out from underneath, that every horror movie has conjured at least once, always fills my head as I stand near the car loading the trunk. It is the same reason I had to check every stall before settling on one in a public restroom. Horror movies told me to.

The longest part of leaving our new "neighborhood" is the trip around the crypts and to some resemblance of an actual road. We park the car behind the long rows, hoping to keep it hidden and never directly behind our actual crypt. I try to rotate where we park to avoid tire tracks or other obvious signs for someone to notice. I never take the same path out either for the same reasons. Genny loves to make paranoia jokes over my actions, but monsters come in many forms these days and my paranoia is what may just keep us safe.

The road to town becomes worse to see with each venture back into where the population once dominated. What once granted the memories of a war scene now resembles an apocalypse. The cars and roads gain the layers of the seasons with amber colored leaves and smudged dirt. The cars are lanes deep from the traffic jam that resulted in the panic to escape the debris from the open windows and doors. The corpses left sitting or slumped in their cars now rot from decay. Some show signs of animal scavenging with exposed bones or discarded limbs. At least, I like to tell myself it is all from animals and not from worse things that could be waiting.

It is hard to see our town like this. Memories of smiles and sunny days conflict with the images our eyes hold. Genny sinks lower in her seat with each cluster of death we come across as her own memories are invaded.

Our town was a small, close-knit population. It was a type of place where young kids were safe to play in the many parks that were placed in neighborhoods. Libraries and locally-owned burger joints were the popular hangouts for teens. Our coffee shops were small business not generic chains and the women would gather around farmers' markets to gossip rather than large retail stores. Our high school football games brought in people from miles around. You would've thought the pro-leagues played at our high schools for as much attention as our kids received. "Small Town Hero" was not just a slogan here. It was once a birthright.

The draw back with such a small town is the supply for demands. Hurricanes were prepared for at the first sight of the circling mass on the news, not when the long, stringy lines of forecasted maps brought it our way. Cold and flu season's needs were stocked the day after the first freeze. When real disasters struck, it was our neighbors who we each turned to for help, rounding out what was lacking in exchange for promising to do the same for another. It was an unspoken vow. When your neighbors become what you are hiding from, there is no help and the "Small Town Heroes" are always the first to fall.

We run the risk of being spotted if we travel too closely to town. The major stores already have been destroyed, leaving the main streets resembling something from a war-torn country. Streets are normally filled with the conquerors, standing still like storefront mannequins, keeping watch over their victories. Tragedies bring out the true nature of a person. So far, all I have encountered from our noble town people is panic and hate. Neither makes for a good traveling partner.

Here on the backside of town, the roads are less horrific. A few mangled vehicles stand stationary, left where they collided against trees or other vehicles. Thankfully, they are empty of their owners' remains. It is almost peaceful here and it is sad that as I pass through the wreckage of people's lives I can think that.

Pulling the car around to the back of the store's parking lot, I wait with the engine running. Holding my breath, I struggle with my panic as I strain to notice any movements that will signal we have been followed. Genny's and Ginjer's heads pivot, staring out the windows on their sides as they too scan the area around us. With only silence and the songs of birds still playing from the trees, we exit the car sending out silent prayers for our safety.

Please Lord, don't let my daughter see me die today. I chant mentally, hoping someone up there is still listening and all of this is not a form of a recreation for them like some twisted style of stress relief.

Footsteps fall in behind me and I mentally pull my big girl panties on. I will need them when they discover where we are "shopping." I can already mentally hear the moaning from each of them, but for different reasons. I am about to push the comfort level for them both to the extreme.

Genny hands me the crowbar, with which I have become quite resourceful, when we reach the back metal door. Normally, I would try to peek into any windows to gain a better idea of what is waiting for us. Sometimes, I will break one to see if it stirs any response before I allow us to enter. Today any such action will alert the two behind me to where we are. I am trying to avoid that melt down for as long as possible.

The door gives with a popping and a metallic moan. My senses are so heightened with my nervousness that the door may as well have screamed with pain. Crouching low, I stare into the darkness, letting my eyes adjust before fully entering. What I see makes me wish I had listened to the better half of my brain and avoided this place.

The painted walls are lined in a "L" pattern with metal cages stacked two high around a tiled floor. Different sizes of pillows with prints of cartoon bones are placed on the floor along the opposite wall. Leashes of various brightly colored materials are attached to the silver locks that slide into place and keep their visitors secure.

Black vacant eyes stare at me in various shapes and sizes from behind the bars. The smell of their dead bodies rushes to me like an ocean's wave and it buckles my knees with its strength. I choke and sputter with as much distress as if the wave was water shoved down my lungs instead of the scent of so many rotting dogs that were left behind in the desperation to flee.

The smell of their waste rolls into the scent of their deaths inventing layers of destruction to my senses. My eyes water with the acidic foulness and my sorrow over the sight. My stomach clenches, threatening to lose the meager meal it holds from breakfast. The muscles in my body feel loose, leaving me unsteady and unsure if I want to signal for those outside to follow me. It would be simple for me to run in the doggie daycare/pet store and grab the items I am hoping they have, sparing them from seeing this.

"Mom, what is that smell?" At least, it would be if Genny wasn't always one step directly behind me. I watch as the revulsion sweeps over her. Her eyes dart from cage to cage seeing the discarded contents left within them. She takes note of the few cages where the doors appear to be chewed and bent with attempted escapes. I can see her heart breaking on her face and mine echoes her emotions.

"Tell Ginjer to stay outside. We don't need her to see this." I let my voice hold the smallest thread of volume, but it is enough.

I listen as Genny gives the duty of keeping an eye out to the woman. It allows her to think she is doing us a favor by staying outside versus us doing her one by keeping her out. Of course, she is flattered by our appreciation of her skills and wonders why it has taken us so long to see them. To all of this, I just shake my head as their voices float back into the room.

With a spare chewed shoe that was left by the door, we prop it open just wide enough to allow us to hear if our names are called. Genny, keeping her eyes down, follows in my wake without asking any questions. The bags make rustling noises in the too silent space, hampering my straining ears to hear the slightest twitch of a warning. The sound of buzzing flies as we creep deeper into the room forces me to swallow against my stomach's rebellion. Genny begins to dry heave behind me as the room begins to overtake her.

I offer her an escape from this torment. "Do you want to wait outside?"

Her ponytail swishes rapidly back and forth with her negative response to my question. She isn't brave enough to test her voice. Who am I to argue with her?

The door for the storage room is a basic wooden style lacking a lock. The knob seems to turn agonizingly slow in my nervous hand. Genny's gagging only adds to the imagined hours it takes to open the door. The smell that greets us in this room isn't any better.

At first, the plastic bins on their shelving units send a flutter of hope through my body. With any luck, they will be filled with cans of food and bottles of water. With karma being what she is, they may be filled with squeaky toys and shampoo. When nothing jumps out at us or makes any noise alerting us that we are not alone, I open the door fully and motion for Genny to go past me.

"What are we looking for?" With the dead animals out of sight, her coloring is slowly starting to return.

"Food," I say to her, and instantly regret it.

Her jaw drops with exaggerated teen angst. "You can't be serious? You want us to eat dog food?"

"Some of this stuff is better prepared than anything I could have ever cooked for you before any of this started. Don't think of it as "dog food" think of it as… "stew." I try to offer her any mental help I can give her to overcome this imagined insult. Unfortunately, the reality is that food is becoming harder to find, but if the bins along the back wall of the room mean anything, this "stew" isn't.

Seven bins sit labeled, hinting at their contents and finally I feel as if our luck might be changing. Unzipping the first of our bags, I quickly rip open the lid of a bin with my excitement. What I see is better than pots of gold. It is filled with tall round cans that shine under my flashlight with their colorful paper wrapping boasting about the minerals and vitamins held within. Can after can of beef, chicken, turkey, and even some seafood variations are tossed into bags with mixed reactions. The last three bins contain bottles of water for the clients that prefer their animals not drink from the tap. Which always amuses me since dogs will drink from a toilet if left to their own devices. This may not be the gourmet meals of dried jerky and fruit-roll ups she has become used to the last few days, but I know once she gets past the idea of what it is, the battle will be won.

"Mom," Genny's voice holds the tremble of fear and it pulls me out of my mental victory. My eyes follow where she is staring and my heart drops into the pit of my stomach before returning to sit in my throat with a nauseating bounce.

At the edge of the shelving unit, tucked back into a far corner, sits a woman, slumped and brittle. Her blonde hair hangs loose around her face, blanketing her features. She wears pastel scrubs with embroidered cartoon dogs dancing around the name of the business. One foot sits bare of a shoe, the delicate, high-gloss mauve toenails reflect the light from our flashlights. I guess that answers as to why one shoe was left by the door.

"Is she…" Genny trails off her thought, letting her voice carry the question when her words cannot.

"She's dead," I tell her, exhaling the breath I was not aware of holding.

"They all *look* dead." She tells me this, as if I have not been with her this whole time, watching and learning right along with her.

"She's dead," I tell her again. A little more firmly this time, praying she won't push the matter.

"How-" she starts and I sigh, letting the beam of my flashlight travel the length of the wall behind the woman. The new red layer of dried paint tells the truth of what has happened in the back of this supply closet. There are a thousand reasons why someone would take this way out. I only have one reason to keep going.

"Let's go. I don't want to leave Ginjer alone too long."

With our bags loaded, and with food now for at least another month, we make our way past the woman to the exit.

"Go on," I tell Genny, waiting until she is out of sight to kneel down and pry the revolver from the woman's hand. Her fingers are stiff and the snapping sounds make me gag with each pop of her knuckles. If you had asked me three months ago if I could ever picture myself surviving the end of the world, I would have laughed at the thought. Right now after stealing a gun from a corpse's hand and toting bags of dog food, this shit isn't so funny.

The sunlight blinds me for a moment when I exit the building. The smell of death and decay follows me like a cloud to the car where they are packing the bags already. Genny is still coughing as she tries to fight back the nausea, and when our eyes meet, all I have to offer her is a pat on the shoulder and another layer of guilt to my soul.

"I think I saw one of those quickie mart pharmacy things on our way here. We should stop in." Ginjer smiles as if this is a "girl's day out" and she is adding another shopping detour to our plans.

"No, we got what we came for. We should go back before our luck runs out." I hold the same tone I use when Genny is asking for the moon and she knows it's not possible. I hope that the same subtle message will work for Ginjer.

"There is no one for miles. We'll be fine. You're just being paranoid, again." She actually smiles and winks at me. My grandmother used to have a saying for women like her, "Bless her heart because her mind is gone."

"Ginjer, we are not going to risk it. One trip a day. It has always been the rule." I settle into the seat of the car leaving no room for debate, but I don't anticipate who would join in on the argument.

"Mom, let's just check it out. I could use a few things, too." I would have left Ginjer on the side of the road before giving in to her demands, but the fragile voice of my daughter throws all of the rules right out the window.

She sits in the back seat, hugging herself, staring at her feet intently as if they have suddenly become very interesting. Another layer of guilt and another rule broken, but what can I do?

"Alright," I sigh. "Alright, but in and out. No lingering." At least, I will try to pretend to hold on to the illusion that I am still in charge.

Chapter 6

The store Ginjer had spotted was once a mom-and-pop deal that supplied the basics of prescriptions, the basics of needs and the basics of accessories. Basically, the basics of hopes for nice retirement checks and maybe a family legacy. I don't suppose either of those really matter anymore.

The store lot is covered with the litter of past lootings. It swirls with the leaves in the wind when the fall weather blows across the asphalt. There are no other cars parked near the store. There is no movement signaling we have alerted anything or that there is anything to alert. Still, something just doesn't sit right with any of it. Maybe I am too paranoid.

"So..?" I hear Genny's annoyed voice behind me. She has gone from sullen to full frustration while she waited. I know she is looking for someone to be angry with about what happened to the animals. I'm just the lucky one to be near her.

"Just stay close," I say to her, with hopes that she will listen; high, sinking hopes.

My knees almost shake as we enter the store. The little brass bell that was once the owners' idea of security softly chimes refusing any attempts to enter unnoticed. As our eyes adjust, the scene before us is depressing in a different manner. Litter from discarded items is strewn about, layering the once pristine shop with trash. Shelves are knocked askew, if not completely turned over, spilling what they once held around them. Registers are broken and smashed, robbed of their contents as if cash holds any value now. I can only hope that the owners never had to see their "baby" in such a disarray.

"So, what are we looking for?" I ask, as if finding anything in this place will be possible.

Genny grumbles something under her breath and heads off into what once served as the feminine hygiene section. *Good to know that we can stake monsters in the head, but we still can't hold a conversation about your period, Genny girl.* I smile with the thought. No matter how things change, some things will always be the same.

Ginjer strolls along the destruction, smiling like she is cruising a designer shop. Her fingertips tap along the items left on the shelves as she tilts her head side-to-side comparing items before tossing them into her purse. A part of me has to wonder what freedom she is now enjoying with society's rules thrown to the wind. *Bless her heart…*

I leave Ginjer to her afternoon klepto-fest to check on Genny. The store being small and a basic rectangle makes it easy to keep the whole view in sight. There are no corners to hide around and with most of the shelves being knocked down, it is even easier to spot any dangers. Unless something is crawling on its belly towards you, there is really no risk of being ambushed. The thought pulls my head down to my feet with mental panic and I have to laugh at my foolishness. Just call me the Queen of Paranoia Land.

"Find everything?" Genny jumps with my voice and turns hostel eyes to me.

"Really, Mom?"

She quickly shoves the remaining boxes of products into her bag while glaring at me. The pretty shade of pink she is turning robs her of the full effect of her annoyance. Any other day I would have had a little fun teasing her about her "purchases," but with her anxiety already a full ten on the scale, I give her a little breathing room.

"You ready?" Ginjer stands behind me with a smile that a lipstick company would covet. "Let's go."

er eyes are a little too wide. Her voice is a little too happy. My stomach just became a little too anxious.

I arch an eyebrow, asking for a hint or a clue for her behavior. Keeping her smile frozen on her face, she shakes her head with a subtle movement.

"Let's go," she repeats, a little more 'happy' this time.

"I'm afraid I can't let you do that." With the sound of the male voice behind me, my stomach drops while my pulse rises.

I pivot to see every mother's nightmare. The man holds my daughter with a one-arm embrace, pulling her backwards as he walks. Without a thought, I follow them just as he intended. Genny's eyes are wide and pleading with me silently for any help, her feet slipping over the objects littering the ground and her legs shaking from fear. I am angry at myself for letting my guard down and allowing my daughter to fall target to danger. I, in my naivety, had thought this place safe while inside I had sensed something was wrong from the start.

"Sit," he tells me, motioning with his head to the wall beside him.

No way, Jose.

"You don't have to do this. We don-," I begin to explain, but he cuts my sentence short with his voice.

"Sit," he tells me again, jerking Genny tighter against him and letting his threat sink in.   Okay, Jose.

Ginjer and I slide down the wall until we are sitting like good little captives. He hands Genny a roll of thick tape, pushing her forward to us. Her hands shake and she stands still, mute and unsure of what he wants.

"He wants you to tape our hands." I hold my arms out to her, wrists together, praying that if I assist he will leave my daughter alone. I want her closer to me, not him.

"..and feet. Tape their feet, too." The man sounds as unsure of his plans as Genny is of what to do, and I lose a few inches of my apprehension over him.

Genny is sniffling as she winds the tape with uneven circles around my wrists, but she is refusing to cry. With her mind focused on the job, she is no longer looking to me for guidance and I can stare at the man that paces the floor in front of us.

With one hand brought to his mouth to chew a thumbnail, and the other rubbing the back of his neck, he holds no weapon that I can see. His head is downcast, heavy with his thoughts. He is dressed in basic jeans and tee-shirt with running shoes on his feet. Markings along his wrists show signs of having just removed a jacket telling me that he has not been inside the store long. This isn't a kidnapping. This is a botched supply run, just like ours.

Trying to reason with him, I keep my voice calm and an even pitch, "Look, we don't know you and you don't know us," I tell him. His pacing hinting that he is just as nervous about his actions as we are. "We will sit here, count to ….twenty…and we will never see which way you go or remember anything about you. There is no need to hurt anyone."

He stares at me with dark colored blue eyes. They are filled with an emotion that contradicts his actions.

"I just need to think…" his voice trails off, as he stares at the ground, seeking answers for questions that only he can hear being whispered in his mind.

Still clutching the tape in her hands, Genny sits beside me trying to avoid his scattered focus. I turn my upper body, placing my taped wrists over her body, attempting to shield her and pull her closer to me.

"My name is Beth. This is my daughter, and this is my friend. What's your name?" His eyes slowly float to me with confusion over my question. "Normally, I prefer dinner and a movie before I let a guy tie me up, but a name would suffice given the circumstances."

He smiles at me before he catches himself. With that small action, I know that this is not a criminal mastermind at work. Just a guy, in the wrong place at the wrong time, just trying to survive, just like us. Our odds just increased by metric tons in my mind.

"Collin?" The man's head snaps up with the new voice from the back of the store.

By his reaction, I guess we have answered the name debate.

He darts his eyes in our direction with almost fear building in them. He points at me before heading towards the voice, keeping his wide eyes on me with another silent threat and message. Unfortunately for him, I don't take directions well and I am not about to just sit here until he comes back.

"Get it off," I tell Genny, who is already pulling at the bindings of the tape. Male voices hiss in whispers that carry the conversation to us in disjointed fragments as Genny fights with the tape. Her hands shake with her nerves, making our escape clumsy and frantic.

With my hands free, Genny moves to help Ginjer and I begin to unbind my legs. I keep my attention on the whispered hissing during our escape. I know as long as they are whispering, they are not paying attention to what we are doing. My heart thumps at the risk of being discovered. Collin may not be a threat, but his partner might be.

With silent nods we begin to stand, crouching low to keep our heads hidden, as we make our way to the front of the destroyed store where our freedom waits.

"Hey…" I cringe hearing the new voice take notice of us, but shove Genny forward anyway.

"Go," I tell her, praying this man also doesn't have a weapon. There is no longer a need to crouch and we begin to run to the door as fast as the obstacle-laden floor allows.

"Wait! Wait, please!" the other man shouts at our backs, and I have to laugh at the idea. "We need help…" his voice trails off, sinking in pitch at our departure. He sounds defeated and saddened, pulling on a cord in me that forces my body to slow against my will.

You have got to be kidding me, a part of me thinks even as I turn to glance at him. His hands are held in the air, palms out, with either a gesture of pleading or a show of peace. His body language belongs to someone that has taken on a heavy burden and is wearing thin with the duty. His long-sleeved shirt is stained with irregular dark patterns with what my mind screams is blood. It's his eyes though that pull at me with their dark depths of sorrow. *You have got to be kidding me*, I scold myself again, but I already know what is about to happen.

"Mom!" Genny urges me forward sensing my inner debate.

"Please…," the man calls again, and I am torn between the need to get my daughter to safety and the human nature that I still claim. Ginjer stands behind me wearing the same look of shock and incredulousness as Genny over what I am about to do.

"Shit," I sigh under my breath, hating a part of me. It is a red-letter type of day for breaking rules. Give me a giant red 'R' and let's get it over with. "What?" My voice holds no offer of friendship and I am ready to run out the door with the slightest hint of trouble.

"It's my son. He's just a kid. We need help." The man may as well have shot me on the spot. His words are just as dooming to my fate. How does a parent turn away from a hurt kid? How can anyone for that matter?

Chapter 7

After a brief introduction of the two men, I reluctantly drive to follow them with a mental mantra of how stupid I am. We discover who their group is and where they have been waiting for their return. It's a row of vehicles parked deep along a dirt trail in the wooded area behind the store. A few cars and a very southern Jeep hold passengers with weary eyes and clamped lips. If this is their 'welcome wagon' I would hate to see their 'angry townsfolk' routine.

Collin and the man who had earlier introduced himself as Terrence exit from their car, heading into the line of stone-faced watchers. I watch their brief exchange with the others and squirm a little, rethinking my decision, as their heads turn toward us.

"Why did you tell them you were a nurse back at the store, Ginjer?" I look to the woman beside me trying to remove myself from the stares.

"I never said how good of a nurse I was." She shrugs with this comment, watching the crowd in front of us.

"I think they are expecting a pretty decent nurse." Even Genny's snarky comment shows how worried she is about what this could mean when they discover the woman's ruse.

"I know the basics. I doubt anyone needs brain surgery here." Once again, another shrug and I feel like Ginjer just enjoys seeing how far my patience level can be pushed.

"I dropped out of school after meeting my husband. I know enough and what I don't know, I'll bluff." She smiles as if this all makes a perfect plan. I think I will keep the car running just the same.

Genny, the lover of all things books, asks with genuine interest, "Why did you drop out?"

"The money was better to be married," Ginjer tells us this as if it should obviously answer any questions we may have. In a way, it does.

Collin is staring at us with confusion, and points to the back of the Jeep. The 'town folk' aren't confused, but they are staring just as hard.

"I hope your acting skills are better than your cooking," I mutter to her, as I exit the car. There are a thousand ways this could go wrong. We only need one to put us back at risk and that one exits the car beside me.

"They can't be any worse than your cleaning skills." Ginjer gives me one of her southern, socialite smiles and leads us to the waiting group.

"When did she get so lippy?" I try to encourage a smile from Genny when she exits the car. Forging through a room of dead dogs, discovering a woman who committed suicide, and being taken hostage only to end up willingly at their camp has to be the definition of a bad day.

"You know this could go very badly?" Genny asks, holding my hand as we walk, needing the touch of reassurance.

"If it does," I slip the car keys into Genny's purse with my words, "you get out of here."

"Why do all of your plans involve me leaving you?" My daughter turns to me with an annoyed expression over a question I think the answer to is rather obvious.

"Because you are my daughter and nothing is more important to me than your life, but the next time I say we are skipping a store, we are skipping the damn store." I touch my forehead to hers with our private conversation, hoping to share a smile. It is a brief flash of a grin, but I will take it. Beggars can't be choosers and right now I am begging for this to turn out right.

Terrence's son has a long gash on his left calf. His pants have been cut up the seam to expose the wound that lies bleeding into the once white towels that brace his leg. The flesh is jagged and torn framing a wide, perfect arch where the pieces have been removed. The skin around the wound shows signs of scraping with thin ribbons of blood beading along the lines. His skin tone is grey and pale from the pain and nausea that he is suffering. His blonde hair cut is in the typical teen windblown bowl look that many young stars brought back to popularity. Strands of his bangs are matted and stuck to his forehead with his moist perspiration. Terrence clutches his son's hand in a white-knuckle fist, pulling it to his chest. He whispers words of encouragement, trying to soothe the teenage boy while staring at Ginjer with hopeful eyes.

Ginjer swallows against the sight of the wound, blanching for a moment, but when she feels the many eyes staring at her, the curtain rises. Her perfect socialite smile pulls her lips up at the corners. Her head cocks and she begins to make soothing noises as if she were suddenly possessed by Mother Teresa herself.

A woman, who has admitted many times to hating kids, sometimes wishing them brutal harm for their antics, now stands examining a wound that stains her elegant fingers. Her brow furrows with the medical concerns I know she is lacking. I find myself forgetting her admitted secret as I watch her and wonder what else she has hidden from us. Her flip from the demanding and pampered to this resolved survivor with all of her social trappings stripped from her today makes me wonder who is the real Ginjer.

"We have the stuff for stitches, but nobody here knows how to do them." Terrence hands what looks like a battered tackle box to Ginjer. Inside are many different compartments and tiers that have been converted for medical needs. They are segregated and sectioned into areas, clumping together items depending on the needs they would best serve.

Bandages, gauze and paper tape room together in one tier. Prescription pills with their amber-colored plastic bottles rattle against one another on a higher tier. A collection of fishing hooks that have been stretched and converted into needles with the matching twine nestle in the last compartment. My stomach flutters realizing what she is going to have to do.

"We will need to clean it. Stitching a wound that has been open this long can become infected. Who knows what bacteria are already in there." Ginjer's voice is steady and secure in her knowledge. Once again, I have to stare at this woman, wondering who she really is.

"We are running short on water. Is there any other way?" The look that Ginjer gives one of the townsfolk with his question is not a kind one.

"Genny, I think we might have something in the car." I let the words drag, hoping she catches my meaning without revealing too much information about our supplies. These people look worn and haggard. I don't really want to get into a fight over dog food. My bullshit meter is filled already today.

When Genny returns with an opened, misused, half-filled bottle of water, I have to bite my smile. She caught on perfectly and understood the risks of returning with anything that might gather more suspicions.

Ginjer smiles when she sees the bottle, but quickly masks it as one of appreciation.

"This will do perfectly," she tells Genny, exchanging our secret with her smile.

Ginjer has rubbed a packaged alcohol prep swab over her hands and dragged the needle she selected to use with the fishing twine through another. The kid's eyes roam from the needle waiting on the swab to Ginjer with unmasked fear.

"This is going to hurt." Terrence pulls his son's upper body against his chest to help brace the boy. It does nothing to settle the fear in the boy's eyes.

Without a word spared, Ginjer begins to pour the water over the wound. It may as well have been molten lava by the way the boy clenches his teeth and exhales his misery. She alternates between pouring the water and pressing against the wound, releasing new blood to flow with hopes of expelling anything that may set an infection. Terrence's arms bulge, defining each muscle with the act of holding his son still. We are all lost in his misery, forgetting the risk his loud moans may present.

Pinching the wound together so that the edges are aiming outward, Ginjer pushes the needle through. The thread appears to be connected to the boy's stomach. With each puncture, he hisses in pain and with each pull, he gags with the length of the thread that is sliding through his skin. She pulls the thread just tight enough to hold the wound's edges together with each steady stroke and ties a knot on one side of the wound, never on top, repeating until the wound is closed. With the final knot in place, she and Terrence both exhale the breath that I bet neither of them were aware that they were holding.

With the leg stitched and bandaged, both the boy and his father start to regain their normal coloring. Ginjer accepts the smiles and pats on the back with extreme grace, never letting on to the truth. She is calm and collected, appearing as if she never had a doubt the outcome would be positive. Glad one of us didn't.

"Beth?" The voice only proves that today is full of surprises, and I spin to be sure of what I am hearing. I return the shocked smile of the woman who has been my "partner in crime" for the past many years.

"Aunt Alicia?" Genny's nerves have hit their brick wall and this new discovery frees all her tension that has been building with today's events in an explosion of emotion. She forgets her teen dignity with its perfect aloofness and runs into my sister's arms. They stand, rocking with their embrace, celebrating in a rare moment in this new life: happiness.

"Who is that?" Ginjer asks of me, unhappy that she is no longer the center of the attention she had gained.

"My Guardian Angel." Is the only response that I seem to find fitting at this moment.

"Who?" Ginjer misses both the point and the moment with her cold eyes gazing at whom she perceives as a threat to her imagined crown.

"My sister. She's also Genny's God Mother. We even went to college together." She is many things, and I stand patiently awaiting our moment letting Genny take all the comfort that she needs.

"You went to college?" The shock in her voice does not dampen my mood as I realize the show is over and the woman I have come to know is back.

Her flippant demeanor will not take this moment from me. I watch my daughter lost in her joy. She has lost her father, her friends and her way of life, but she has never given up. She has fought and killed to survive to stand here today. We have spent nights huddled together, our stomachs a pit of dread and starvation, praying to make it through to the morning.

We have watched houses burn and people kill each other for something as simple as a box of crackers. Never, never has she given up though.

My cheeks grow wet with my tears as I watch them whispering and embracing, lost in the miracle of finding each other. Alicia and I had become better friends in college than we had our whole lives. We were both lost and out of our league at the local university. For both of us, college was something of a dream for our family. It was a fantasy and a threat of bankruptcy to our middle class life-style. We had both earned scholarships and worked part time jobs to make our dreams come true, determined to live better lives than our parents. With as much as we had in common, we also had a part.

Alicia, with her cluster of Daddy issues, seemed to like men who were unobtainable. The harder the romance was to reach, the harder she burned for it. Whereas I, a Dear Diary of my own 'Daddy' issues, preferred men who were safe and secure and ones who were almost boring. It always started the same for me. A few romantic dates would soon simmer, resulting in us reaching the 'friend zone,' before finally ending with our false promises that we would keep in touch. I never kept in touch and the colder my flames became the hotter hers burned.

We stayed close after we crossed that stage. She was my Maid of Honor when I married Charlie. She was the first person in the hospital room after Genny's birth. She was the supplier of cookie dough and chick-flicks when the divorced was settled. There has not been a day when I have not prayed that she was safe somewhere. I guess someone is still listening, after all.

Their eyes turn to me and I go to them. We don't speak. We just embrace in our gratitude for finding each other, a small part of our souls heal from the suffering we have faced.

"All this time…," Alicia's voice is soft with wonder, "I kept hoping I would find you. I kept looking, but after all this time. After all this time I just gave up." Her voice cracks. The guilt and grief she has been holding inside of her is too much for her to not convey. "I went by your house," she continues, "but it was all gone. The whole street looks as if it fell to madness or bombs. Hell, maybe both. Houses were burned or gutted; just destroyed. It was unbelievable."

"I was hoping you had stayed on your trip far away from here," I say to her. "Maybe on some tropical island with a nice umbrella drink. Dancing with the dark-skinned, male natives."   I smile at her but my resolve is breaking with my sister's strength faltering beside me. I'm not alone anymore and that realization tears down the false strength I have been hiding behind.

"I wish." She tries to smile but her face slides back into the creases her frown leaves. "I came back the day it happened. If you think flying was bad before, you should see how long check-in lines become when people start dropping." She means it as a joke, but the laughter doesn't reach her eyes.

"How did you find us?" Alicia asks. She is still clutching Genny to her, refusing to release her, too afraid of her vanishing like the ghost of a dream. It is evident in the way she strokes Genny's hair, leans her cheek against the top of Genny's head and whispers soothing words to her in-between our conversation. Which is why when Genny tells her how we made it here, she explodes.

"He tried to kidnap me," Genny volunteers. All of the energy is gone from her voice. Like the eyes belonging to a painted doll, her eyes stare blankly from today's stress at the man who helped cause it. A man who just happens to be unfortunately standing across from us, Collin.

Alicia pauses for a moment, unsure of what she heard before turning to me to confirm the story. Knowing my sister well, I reluctantly nod and brace for a heat wave of anger.

"It was a misunderstanding," Collin volunteers and accepts the blame for what has happened. He is either very brave or just wishing for his life to end. I know the wrath of Alicia. With as much as his actions anger me, I almost pity him for what is to come.

"You. Did. What?" Each word is clipped and short, her anger, and the target for it, evident with her teal-green eyes glaring. Her arms bind Genny closer to her, protecting her now from what she was not able to before.

"I didn't know who they were. I didn't know what to do," Collin pleads his case, but when Alicia's eyes are this green, the best thing he can do is cower and apologize. Alicia's anger is the perfect example of why men are taught to just answer "Yes, Dear," and walk away, slowly.

"You didn't know that a teenage girl and two women couldn't overpower you and Terrence? That says a lot about you, don't you think?" Alicia's words are biting and he winces from the verbal slap.

"I didn't tie *her* up." Collin tries to better his story while pointing to Genny.

"He had me put the tape on Mom and Mrs. Ginjer after dragging me through the store to make them follow us."

I don't know if my daughter is seeking some form of payback, or if she's just not aware of how well she is stirring the pot now with her answers. Watching Alicia's face, we are all very aware. The pot is stirred and boiling over.

If anger had a shade, it would not be red. I have seen enough red to know what the shade belongs to and why we fear that shade. No, if anger were a shade it would be the color of Alicia's eyes, because looking into them now there is no question about her thoughts. The peaceful teal-green has slowly deepened into the color of a green so dark it almost appears black with her anger.

I watch all of Collin's bravery slip from him with a sigh. I have a sense that he has seen this side of her before with how easily he gives over to her anger. Watching her mood deepen, he has switched to the gear of self-preservation instead of defending his actions. His head bows sideways as he waits for her verbal explosion like a child knowing they have done wrong and their punishment is coming.

"We have rules in this group. Rules Peyton has made to keep ourselves safe and any others that we may find safe. One of those is that we do not hurt innocent people to further our causes. We especially do not take advantage of children! It's bad enough you left your own children to die, but now you have to harm another's, too."

Her words are like heat-seeking missiles and they find his heart like the weapon they were intended to be.

I don't know the man's story, or what his real relationship is with Alicia. I do notice by the spasms of emotions on his face that she knows him well enough to know exactly what to say to wound him mortally. The whispering murmurs around us shame him further with his hinted backstory.

"Who's Peyton?" Genny resembles a china doll with her pale skin tone and blank wide eyes. Hiding in the security of Alicia's arms, she seems just as fragile.

"I am and I'd like a hint as to what is going on here." Peyton is leaning on the side of the Jeep watching their little domestic show-and-tell and at the sound of his voice the crowd around us disperses. It's as if they all suddenly are remembering something very important they have to do. Something that they have to do that will allow them enough distance to be out of the way, but still close enough to pretend they are not listening.

Peyton's stance seems to be relaxed as he stands beside the sleeping teenager and his father, but his face is all for us. His pale colored eyes, showing his age with the slight wrinkles at their edge, pause on each of us as he waits to see which one will speak first. He is wearing a thick flannel shirt with hopes it will reduce the bite of the wind when it blows. The winter's icy fingers are gaining strength as the afternoon sun begins to lose its power.

His jeans are as stained and worn as the rest of ours, showing he is more than battle friendly and well versed in what could be waiting for us at any moment. Yet, with all of this sternness, there is a kindness about him. It is a kindness that comes from understanding and seeing every facet of human nature from having had to shoulder the heavy burden of being a leader.

"Ginjer. With a 'J'." Never missing the chance to be the center of male attention, Ginjer extends her hand to him, forgetting where they just were.

Peyton's eyes flick to her hand before an amused smile becomes his face. His eyes darted to me standing behind her before coming back to Ginjer. Ginjer had tried to clean her hands the best she could after stitching the teen's leg, but there are still smears of blood dried in the crevices of her nails. It is probably not the best seduction technique she has ever planned to date.

"Well Ginjer, with a 'J', I see I have you to thank for Kent's leg." Peyton doesn't take her extended hand, but lets his words explain as to the reason why before she can become offended.

"Yes, sorry, I'm still a bit messy from the surgery." Ginjer doesn't even bat an eye at the exaggeration. "I'm just happy I was here to save him."

Once again, Peyton looks to me with an amused smile from her antics while waiting on my introduction.

"This is my sister, Beth, and her daughter, Genny. Who Collin here thought would be a good idea to try to kidnap and tie-up." Alicia adds honey to her voice, but it's as sweet as acid and burns another layer of dignity from Collin's face.

Ginjer becomes very put-out, almost delicate with her whisper of a voice, "He tied me up, too." She stares at Peyton, waiting on his sympathy with lowered eyes and pouting lips.

"I didn't *tie* them up. I used tape. Well I had Genny use the tape..." Collin's words stall discovering that each one only makes his side of the story bury him just that much deeper into the anger of Alicia.

"Where were you when all of this happened?" Peyton looks to Terrence, avoiding Ginjer and trying to gain more insight of the events that unfolded.

Terrence has remained still, like an animal hiding from a hunter while the conversations have centered around the store run-in. Holding his son's resting body, only the movement of his eyes followed the discussion as if he was watching a verbal tennis match between Collin and Alicia. He never once volunteered any support to his friend, a negative strike in my book, but Collin never threw his name into the fray either. That does say a little something about the type of man Collin might be. Now that Terrence has been directly called out, his mind searches for the right words that may save them both.

"I came in after he discovered them. They were able to free themselves and were on the way out when I asked them for help. They came here on their own accord. I think they knew Collin never really meant them any harm, even with as scared as the girl was." His words are slow with his hopes that each one is the right one as he continues his explanation. "I think Collin was just worried that they weren't alone. We don't normally come across a group of women out on their own. We may not have started out on the best foot, but I am very grateful for your help with my son."

An explanation and a thank you wrapped in one. Terrence is either very good at diffusing situations or he was married at one point. With Ginjer beaming her southern charm in his direction, my vote is both.

"Well Ginjer, with a 'J', Beth and Genny, I am sorry we had to meet under these circumstances. I am afraid we don't have much to offer as far as accommodations, but I'm sure we can offer something to make your car a bit more comfortable." Peyton smiles as my eyebrow arches. I am confused if this is a farewell or his welcome.

"That's how we live now," he says shrugging. "It might not be the Hilton, but it makes it real easy to pack and move should the time come." His smile is soft and almost embarrassed with how little that is left to them.

I look around, really seeing this crew for the first time. Their suffering is a mantle of burdens making their shoulders slump with the weight of it. Their clothing is dingy. The colors the fabrics once held have faded, hanging heavily on their bodies like their grief. Cars have been adorned with sun bleached sheets hanging from windows to provide privacy for their 'homes' like curtains. They are parked like rows of apartments, leaving small spaces between each for mingling and attempts forcomforts with well-used chairs and small cooking grills. Every noise in the wind causes them to startle, only adding to the proof of their new standard of life.

I can feel Ginjer and Genny staring at me, knowing that I am thinking of our safe, secure stone walls and the many crypts left still vacant and available for occupancy. One face holds the fear that I will speak up and the other holds the fear that I will not. It is the same within me.

My heart is afraid I will turn my back on people who I can so easily help. My brain is afraid I will listen to my heart. The 'pros' and 'cons' of both sides is waging war in my mind with an angel and devil style of debate. The arguments fall like toy soldiers with how easy each side wins a battle, adding only to my confusion over what the right choice is with this mental war.

"I appreciate your offer, but I think we can make do." When in doubt, stall, and that is exactly what I do.

"You don't mean that you three are going to go back out there, alone?" Peyton's face may be amused, but his voice proves his shock and disbelief of my answer.

"No, that is not what she means." Alicia's eyes are turned on me now with that vile green tint. "They will stay with us."

"Yes, dear." I smile at Alicia before continuing. "If you think that is best."

The green of her eyes fades as her anger melts from her. She knows the private meaning of that response and my gall at using it on her amuses her.

"Your mother is a very funny woman," Alicia tells Genny, who is finally showing some sign of life in her eyes with our secret and with the hopes of staying. Just a perfect ending to a red letter day.

Chapter 8

At first, I was hesitant about how much I should trust Collin and Terrence. I knew soon after our 'capture' that Collin was not a threat, but a mind can change in an instant when everything is in such short supply. If it wasn't for Terrence calling out for help for his son, I would have not had any second thoughts about leaving them both behind in whatever form of life they had carved for themselves. Seeing him wearing the blood of his own child though turned my head from the fears I felt and left only confusion over moral rights and wrongs. I am filled with them still.

These people need something to cling to again. A life that they can settle into once more providing them with the security they crave. I know that I can offer it to them, but at what risk? Other than Alicia, I don't know these people. How well does she know them even? Is the safety of strangers worth risking the life of my daughter? My head tells me no, but sanity prodded by my guilt won't let it be.

Guilt fills my heart each time I make up my mind to leave them. I wonder what lessons I will be teaching Genny with my actions. Is it worth it to lose our humanity for the sake of our survival? If all social morals are gone, what is there to live for? If humanity falls, are we worth saving?

Will each of us become sectioned off and guarded, daring another to cross what we have declared as ours while supplies grow thinner and thinner? How can we as a race rebuild if we have lost all trust for each other? How will we ever heal from this nightmare if we are determined only to inflict more suffering on each other? Who will be the first to scuff the lines drawn in the sand?

"Really, Mom?" Genny's voice startles me, and she smirks at my reaction. "The notebook, again?

"It helps me to think." I feel embarrassed having to justify my obsession.

Genny had spent the night with Alicia trying to relive old times of sleepovers and late night giggling. It left Ginjer and I alone to our thoughts since neither of us really wanted to talk for fear of what the other was thinking. This morning the same thoughts are still swirling in my mind like the many voices of split personalities I had hoped writing them down would help me solve the debates my mind is holding with itself. Like the fine layer of dust that recoats the shelves after dusting, it turned out to only add more doubts to the many that are already dominating my thoughts.

"What did you and Alicia talk about last night?" I ask, with my goal to redirect the conversation with a little wide-eyed wonder of her night.

"Boys," she tells me, with a smile and I am wishing I had just let her tease me to tears over the notebooks.

"Really? Boys?" I ask, not even trying to hide my disbelief. Just yesterday, we were wading through dead animals, planning escape routes and hoping to survive the night in our cars, but they talked about boys? She is a true teenager at heart and my sister is still the corrupter of minors.

"Mmhmm. Aunt Alicia is 'seeing' the Collin guy. Turns out, they knew each other before all of this happened. I think something pretty epic happened between them with how her mood goes all secretive when we talked about him." Genny shrugs, not aware of the depth of significance her revelation holds for me.

There was more than one reason why I felt Collin was not a real threat yesterday. I may know him. My mind fills with new questions as it races to put the facts together like a marred puzzle whose picture is too blurry to help. "Where is your Auntie Alicia now?"

"Dunno. The Collin guy showed up and asked if they could talk. I heard Dad ask that enough before the divorce to know I did not want to stick around." She holds this conversation casually, as she chews on one of the last bits of jerky that we keep stashed in the car for 'just in case' reasons. Hearing the word divorce still makes me cringe with shame as if there weren't enough things to already make me feel as though I have failed her.

"I know asking you to stay by the car would be a lost cause, but try to not wander around too far. You know how fast things can go wrong." I pat her head and let my eyes try to find my sister. I need confirmation on the past that is whispering to me.

"What about Ginjer?" Genny tends to drop the formal titles when it is just her and I. I used to correct her on it, but with how things are, I'm just glad she even speaks.

"That is what I meant by 'how fast things can go wrong'." I smile at her and she returns it with a bit more of a mischievous flavor.

It doesn't take me long to find Alicia. I stand back and watch her go from car to car checking in on whoever is inside them. She hands out supplies and kind words with the hope of promoting sanity and survival. I always told her she was a natural leader just without the belief in herself to become one. I don't know if it is belief now that inspires her or necessity pulling it from her. With how their eyes follow her, I do know that she has finally found her strengths. Sometimes disasters break people, but sometimes, just sometimes, they refine people. Those people become the heroes that we all need.

"What are you gawking at?" Alicia asks, when heading my way after catching me staring at her.

"Not sure. Last time we saw one another, you were hysterical about your lover not coming away with you on the trip because his wife had a garden party he had to attend. Now here you are helping support a group of people who seem ready to bolt under the covers with every breeze that passes. Mostly, I am just staring at the one woman I have missed the most and prayed to be safe somewhere." My voice cracks with my last few words. I hadn't meant for that to happen. A part of me is still in shock over having her standing here in front of me after all this time.

Knowing her own voice would strain under the stress of her words, we just stand, holding hands and letting the unsaid words flow around us like a well-known melody.

There are times when words aren't large enough to fully capture the meaning of what you are trying to say. Their syllables are not long enough to encompass the length of the emotions you are feeling. This is one of those moments. So we don't even try.

"Where have you been?" Alicia asks me after some time has passed, and we can both successfully talk without falling apart.

"Genny and I went to Ginjer's when the neighborhood started getting rough. At first, it was fine, but once the images started showing on the news, everything just went chaotic." I tell her as my mind refills with the memories of the first lootings on our street.

At first, it was boggling to my neighbors as to the reasons why people would cause such harm when we were told it was a contained threat. We made jokes about 'the crazies' and how easily some people jump to the dooms-day-wagon when trouble happens. As the 'containment' spread faster than the news could keep up with, all chaos ensued with thoughts only of protecting yourself first. Those same neighbors were some of the first to encourage the chaos that overtook our streets after Allen died.

"After that, we had it pretty good for a few months. I think the gate and the distance from town kept most of the early looters away. They quickly spread out though and when the first lootings occurred near us, we decided it was time to leave. From there we just kept moving around." I feel bad about the lie, but I haven't yet had time to come to a conclusion about the choices I want to make. Saying the wrong words with so many in earshot could take the choice from me. "What about you? How did you find these people?" My eyes roam over the 'townsfolk' when I ask her, hoping to find Collin again.

"When everything started at the airport it slowly turned into a scene from a murder thriller. People were running everywhere screaming, begging for help. When the killing started, there were just screams. Everyone was rushing for the front doors being followed by those things. They were picked off like cattle with so many packed into narrow halls. A few of us took off down a different hall. We figured that if we stayed far away from the masses, it would increase our chances to escape. It worked. When we finally reached outside, we all stole different abandoned cabs without any second thoughts. Every time I saw sirens speeding up behind me, I was sure they were coming for me, but each time they zoomed past. I drove all the way back here; never stopping. It was just as bad here by the time I made it, though." She pauses, taking a deep breath before rushing into her next explanation. "After finding what had become of your neighborhood, I had to go find her. I had to know if she was ok. I know it was against all the rules, but I had to. I needed to see my daughter. That is when I found Collin, sitting there in his house."

Genny is right. Alicia becomes very secretive when talking about Collin, but it's not for the reasons Genny assumes. She and Collin have a lot of secrets to keep.

"So, it is him?" I ask her, as the puzzle's picture comes into view.

"Yeah, it's him." She hugs herself with a mixture of sadness and shame over my discovery.

"….and your daughter? Did you find her?" We are whispering now as I tense at the question to which I already know the answer.

"No." It is such a frail whisper from her that the wind carries Alicia's word away as if it were a parent changing a scary subject. It is gone before I can fully think about it.

There is no way to salvage the conversation after that discovery. Words are back to being vague and empty. You might as well as comment on how blue the sky overhead is or your favorite sports team. Anything said now will hold the same transparent conversational value.

"Where is Charlie?" Alicia asks me, attempting to end the stalemate.

It is my turn to turn secretive with the mention of my ex-husband. "Dead."

"Are you sure? He could still be out there. We found each other…" Her words are supposed to be an inspirational pep talk, but I know the truth.

"Yeah, I'm sure." She has revealed her secrets and now she wants mine. Just like the darkness of a room, sometimes not being alone is the only thing that can make secrets bearable.

"You found him already?" She whispers it, her eyes going wide when the thoughts connect themselves like dots on a kid's puzzle to form a bigger picture.

"Yes…" I sigh against the question that I know is next.

"Was he dead?" I can't meet her eyes with the question that she asks me.

"Not when I found him, no." My explanation blooms on her face like a flower. Each petal a wider shock of expression upon her pretty features.

We both stare at my daughter laughing and teasing the boy that is the cause of our arrival. "Does Genny know?"

"Does she look like she knows? I would like to keep it that way. She has enough to upset her now. She doesn't need any more nightmares. Not when they are already so abundant." Alicia nods in agreement with me as we listen to the teens' laughter carried to us by the early winter wind. A sound that I thought I would never hear again.

"Well, you up for a run?" Alicia's eyes almost sparkle with mischief, changing the subject at hand.

"I was never much of a jogger before…" I know what she means, but I am hoping she is as easily distracted with my horrible idea of humor as is my daughter.

"Who was? We have all learned how to haul ass now, though." The truth of her words makes me smile. "Whenever we come to a new area, Peyton wants to scout it to see what is where. Supplies. People. Other things…" Her voice falls when speaking of "other things" with no real idea of what to label them.

"Is that how his leg got hurt?" I ask, as we watch the boy limp around, following behind Genny in conversation and movement.

"I'll come get you when we are ready." She walks away before I can ask anything more about the injury. "Don't look so glum. I'll make sure you're in my group."

She smiles at me as she walks backwards away from me.

"Do I get to use the tape on Collin?" I tease her, thinking I will stun her into submission.

"He prefers handcuffs."

I forgot with whom I was playing. "Yeah, that mental image will not encourage me to save his life if the shit hits the fan." I smirk at her, letting her know that she wins.

With a laugh, she leaves me standing with my thoughts as she goes to find out the day's plans. I don't want to help these people, or gain attachments to them. Watching Genny with her new friend, someone finally of her age, I know the risk I am running already.

We will not be able to pick or choose who we invite to break off with us. It will be an all or no one kind of deal. Our lives hang like a feather in the wind already. It sways higher or lower depending on the forces it is under, blowing in complete confusion with no control over where each new sway will take it. As it stands, we have been able to live under the radar with people still clinging to their programming of avoiding cemeteries. If we were to bring 'home' so many new people, will that last? The more there are the more of a risk there is to being discovered and I am really not that sure yet I want to take the risk.

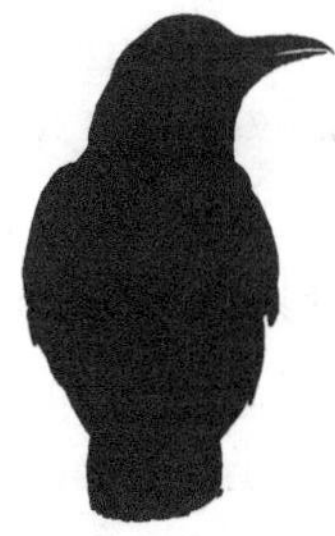

Chapter 9

Peyton did indeed want to scout the area. With the way the announcement caused a rush of worried whispers, I once again wonder what the real story is with the boy's leg. The way their eyes all eventually come to stare at him, I become very curious. I watch as Genny unconsciously steps closer to the boy, her eyes set with determination to battle their stares and my heart sinks some.

"Looks like someone has a new boyfriend." Ginjer smiles at me, teasing me, as if we should be celebrating this fact.

"Yeah, thanks for saving him." My whispered comment draws the attention of the 'townsfolk' closest to us. I arch my eyebrows at their looks making them turn away.

"We'll see, but I doubt it would have been the untreated wound that killed him," she says to me with guarded meaning. "Maybe we shouldn't encourage their friendship."

"Do you see me dropping rose petals or lighting candles here?" Once again, heads turn and I return their stares. "There is not a whole lot I can do about it. Want me to send her to her room?"

"Can't you control your own kid?" Ginjer's complaint pulls a side of me forward, that I am not proud to own.

Says the woman who has only had the desire to raise a dog." I regret it as soon as it slips from my lips. "Ginjer, I'm sorry. I know how much he meant to you."

"No, you're right. What do I know?" The tilt of her head shows me that she is no longer interested in talking with me. Honestly, I can't blame her for the cold shoulder, but if one more person turns to look at me, I may take out my frustrations on them.

Peyton has divided up the area on a stolen map from the mom-and-pop store with wide circles. Just as she said, Alicia and I are placed in the same circle outlining a well-known upper class neighborhood with its tall houses and expansive yards. I think I would have rather had the circle with the church with its lesser of a risk inhabitants than a neighborhood that stands a pretty good chance of being filled with something, to say the least. I wonder if it is too late to add items to the "keep an eye out for" list. I could use a little Holy Water or a big bag of common sense.

Bless me Father, for I have gone insane. It's been 24 hours since my last run-in with death. How many Hail Mary's and Acts of Contrition are needed to save me now?

"You ready?" Alicia is anxious with her nervousness, pulling me from my mental ramblings. "The sooner we get out there, the sooner we can return." She didn't have to say it. The thought is written all over her with the way she checks her bags for storage space and the lists of things they need.

"Will Genny be safe here?" I know by watching my daughter, and being accustomed to her 'save the world' behavior, that she will not want to leave the boy behind. Her halo will compel her to stay here and keep an eye on him since his father is also placed in an exploration group headed to a different circle.

"Yeah. Not many will stay behind. Those that do stay normally sit in their cars to keep the sounds muffled and to be safe from surprise attacks, if it were to happen. We've picked the parking lot of the movie theater up the road to meet up if we get separated." Her eyes never meet mine as she counts wire ties, ammunition, and other various miscellaneous items in her attempt to settle her own nerves. She does nothing to settle mine. "Truth

is, she will most likely be a Hell of a lot safer here than out there with us."
I nod, agreeing with her, but it still doesn't settle my nerves of leaving her.

Alicia is right. The 'other things' don't travel unless they are motivated. We are so far off the main roads. Being surrounded by these thick woods on a dirt road that was once a hunter's trail, that there is no real reason for them to come this way. Where we are going, there are plenty of reasons to find them. After all, there is a chance we are pretty much going knocking on their doors.

"Genny," I call to my child, as I leave Alicia to her military minded madness. For a woman who has always hated the idea of camo, in any color, she has the hunting mentality down. "Genny, I'm going to go help scout out the area with Alicia. Will you be ok here, alone?" I can tell right away that my question has wounded her teen sense of pride.

"Yes, I'll be fine. I know the rules." Her voice is pleasant, but her face is the crowning jewel of annoyance.

"I'll keep an eye on her." Ginjer comes to lean on the side of the Jeep. "I assume she knows 'sit' and 'stay', right?"

I have never seen my daughter and my friend on the same side of the picket line before, much less seen them on the side opposite of myself at the same time. Can't say that I am enjoying it. All I can do is smile and walk away. Being a female, I know that this is dangerous ground and talking is similar to a minefield. You never know which word you step on could be the one word that blows up in your face.

"Thank you, Ginjer." I kiss the top of Genny's head before I walk away and send my silent mantra up to the heavens.

Please Lord, don't let my daughter see me die today.

The ride to our assigned spot is filled with awkward silence with each of us lost in our own fears and mental pictures of what is to come. I never thought about death as much as I do now. I took every day for granted with the monotonous chores that life held. The alarm went off at the same time every day. I went to work on the same road, sat in the same space at the same building, talking to the same people and most times eating lunch at the same place. Death was only a joke then, whereas now, the only punchline that death holds is its own. Death laughs at us now and it has taken back the mantle of terror it should hold.

Our team consists of Alicia, Collin, Peyton and myself. Our sedan is something that would have once been deemed a luxury car with its leather seats and now novelty upgrades. The speaker system it once boasted would be a threat to use now. Its wide body is cumbersome to fit through the many wrecks and hazards that fill the road. The high price name brand means nothing to the things we hide from. It's pure karma that at one time the well-to-do outlives us all with their lifestyle and luxury, whereas now, we blue-collars own the world. What is left of it, anyway.

The road becomes clogged as soon as we find the brick wall built to help reduce the roaring road noise from the first rows of houses. Cars sit with open doors and vacant seats sending ominous emotions through our car. Fall has claimed those parked around us with piles of her leaves, but winter is making her mark as the leaves wither and fade.

Suitcases once packed in haste are opened and scattered around the area. Their items are discarded in random piles, hinting that we are not the first survivors to come this way. Broken bicycles, stripped of their chains and tires, are wedged under cars providing a picture of how this scene started long ago. The area is now deserted, but even with as much as it is hinting at, it still clings to the secret of how it may have ended up this way.

Collin coasts the car past the once cheerful sign advertising the newly-constructed neighborhood. It is eerily calm around us with only lines of well-fed black crows watching us with their cocked heads from rooftops. Sidewalks with their bright, white concrete that was poured for picturesque family walks escort us down the road. Homes stand like bones of a castle with their long, lost memories of times gone by. Their painted doors stand open by force. For some homes, brittle splinters are all that remains from their once secure gatekeepers. Some lawns are filled with destroyed items that may have once been treasures to their rightful owners. Some lawns contain worse.

Human remains with their time worn decay watch us with missing eyes. Their bones are exposed with the damage from weather and scavenging. Jaws lay open as testimonies to their last screams. It is a warning to us as we enter here. These people thought their world was safe and secure only to discover the cruelty of the truth. What makes us think we are any different?

Please Lord, don't let my daughter see me die today.

"Do we have a plan?" I say, and I didn't mean for it to sound as condescending as it did. My mind wanders to my daughter and coats my tongue with bitter emotions from being away from her.

"Most of these houses look ransacked already. I want to drive a little further in just to be sure we are not setting up camp in someone's backyard. We have enough to contend with as it is," Peyton says, and he makes sense. His awareness speaks of some of the possible struggles his group has already faced. Once again, I am reminded of how lucky we are with our row of 'private housing.' It is just depressing that an invaded crypt is now serving as prime real estate for us.

The sights before us do not become any less macabre the deeper we travel. The homes are not as abused but here death is more prevalent. Fallen, destroyed corpses are no longer confined to random locations. They fill the lawns and sidewalks, sometimes in patterns of long rows of bodies laid out under unknown circumstances. The flies are thick like a dark, shimmering haze around the bodies. It is the first hint that not only did these people suffer, but also, they were brutalized.

Some sway from the ropes fastened to the long branches of trees like over ripened fruit. The creaking of the rope is constant like a ticking hand of a clock. The small shapes in faded pastel clothing is indicating that not all were adults when the ropes were placed around their necks. Children with their faces destroyed from decay and animal scavenging stare down at us as we drive past.

"What the Hell…" Collin whispers the words that fill all of our minds.

"Do you see it?" Peyton's voice is forced and humbled.

I don't want to examine the area around us to figure out what it is he has spotted. The images will haunt me with the brief glances I have already taken.

"What do you think it means?" Alicia is watching it all with the silent strength she possesses.

"That there are more forms of madness than we already expected." Peyton's answer causes me to battle against my weakness and once again stare out the window.

I had not seen it before with how I refused to let my eyes rest on any one area too long. Now as I stare into them, I see it. The discoloration around the bodies is not from fall's destruction of greenery or proof of their gory-laden deaths. It is from fire.

"Stop the car," Peyton demands with a voice guarded and tense. "I want a closer look."

Our exit rings out into the silence with the clicking of the car doors. Standing around so much death, and the risk of what did it possibly still lurking somewhere just beyond our sight, sets our nerves on edge. Every crunch that our feet make pulls our eyes to dance around us with trepidation. We follow Peyton not because we share his curiosity. The three of us just don't want to be caught standing alone.

"Look." Peyton points to the first section of bodies lying together in random positions. "The ring of fire never touched them. It's not what killed them."

"Then what is?" Alicia asks, while Collin and I pretend to be keeping an eye on our surroundings. It is better than admitting that we don't have the stomach to explore the question.

"There are holes in each skull." Peyton is moving the decayed heads with the toe of his shoe to examine them, hoping to gain a better idea of what happened here months ago as he walks past them.

"They were shot?" Alicia's voice holds shock and distress. "Why light a ring of fire only to shoot them?"

"The ones in the trees don't appear to be shot." Collin has been staring up, trying to rid his mind's eyes of what is around us. It is a hard task to do with bodies being everywhere.

"There are no children in the circles either. Just in the trees." Alicia's observation does not bring any of us comfort or answers.

"Look," Peyton says again, and I am beginning to dread his observation skills.

He is squatting close to the base of the tree, tracing his fingers through a pattern that has been carved into it. A pattern I have spotted before.

"I saw that when we first came in. It was on the back of the sign, the sidewalk and on some mailboxes." I watch Peyton's face contort with emotions.

"Is it a symbol of some kind?" Collin bends down beside him, curious as what it may mean.

"It is not a symbol. It is letters. Greek letters. IXOYE." Peyton sighs after sharing his revelation. The knowledge it brings him makes his head shake as he stares up into the trees. Tiny shoes sway with a sudden breeze as if excited legs kick with the pieces coming together.

Collin is slowly recovering, like myself, from the sights around us. He grows more curious with his boldness. "What does it spell?" he asks, finally genuinely interested in what is around us.

"Jesus Christ God's Son Savoir." Peyton's voice is weary and disappointed in what we have discovered. "Follow me and I will make you fishers of men."

Alicia no longer hides her shock as she stares at the horror around us. She asks him, "A religious group did this? Why?"

"Why would a religious group claim to do what they do in the name of God? I'm sure the people of Salem would love to have that chat with you." Peyton stands, seeing the area around us with sad, tired eyes.

A new depression has fallen over us. It was one thing to acknowledge the destruction left behind by the events we have all become accustomed to have taken place. There is now a thicker layer of sadness bearing the markings of what humanity has left behind. That is something we had not expected with such a degree of deranged cruelty.

"We aren't going to find anything useful here. These people have been disturbed enough. Dead or not, some things just don't need to be disrespected; even in these times." We agree with Peyton with silent nods and down cast eyes. We return to the car and leave this behind to the nightmare we know is coming for us. Nightmares that will find us tonight filled with the creaking ropes and the bodies of the dead children swaying in the breeze with their tiny shoes and missing eyes.

The ride back is thick with silence. It is heavy and oppressing as if it should hold weight on our shoulders. We each replay what we imagined may have happened to those people like a black and white film. Each time the version is more horrific than the last. In our minds, we don't just hear the creaking ropes, but the screaming also. We see their kicking legs as they choke. We can smell the smoke from the fires. The cries of the tormented begging for their lives fill our minds.

The children in the trees gain faces as we fill the last hours of their lives with imagined mental clarity. Did their necks break or were they forced to hang, kicking and fighting for air? Did their parents watch or were they the ones surrounded by the fire like a private ring of Hell? Where are the rest of the homeowners? Most of all, we are all wondering for what reason did God condemn these people and who carried out His judgements?

What irony would it be if those left to rot, discarded, tortured and forgotten by God's servants are now standing staring down from Heaven, free from this nightmare while God waits for those who misused His name? What injustice would it be if they are not?

Chapter 10

"Are we the first back?" Alicia asks Ginjer, who is filing her nails with boredom. The look she casts Alicia expresses her doubts over the woman's IQ.

"Obviously," Ginjer says, with a hint of bitterness, but when she sees Peyton, her bitterness is dipped in honey. "But I am sure they will be back soon."

As if the universe wanted to prove her right, slowly cars fill the area around us, returning from their trips. Some faces are hollow with the haunting of what they have discovered. Some are void of any signs of emotions, as it is just another day in "paradise" for them. There are returns met with supplies and novelty items met with halfhearted laughter as greetings are exchanged. None of it holds any meaning for me as I still try to hold on to my outsider status, so I search for Genny wanting to hug my own child after seeing the ones that belonged to others.

"She is still with him." Inspecting a nail for imperfections, Ginjer motions with her head. "She has been the whole time. I guess she is happy to find someone to talk with, but I still don't trust him."

"You don't even know the kid." I don't want to take his side. No mother wants to take the side of the other person, but I am right. We don't even know him.

"No, I don't. But I have a pretty good idea of what he will become." Once again, Ginjer leaves me confused by her thoughts, leaving me behind so she may offer Peyton any needed help to take a tally of what was brought back.

I feel almost guilty intruding on Genny when her laughter surrounds me. They are both sitting on the hood of the Jeep, lost in conversation. With my mind constantly on the thoughts of survival, I have taken for granted the need for social aspects of life, too. I am a hamster on a wheel running with all that I am from my fears and just trying to keep us safe. Watching her now, I know there is no backing out from taking them with us and that scares me more than the vision of children swaying in a tree with their bent necks and pointed toes.

"Have fun?" Genny's smile is genuine and full of mirth with her question.

"Barrels," I tell her, noticing the body language in front of me. "Have *you* had fun?"

My question inserts inches between them and a glare from my daughter. The world may have come to an end, but I can still suck the fun right out of an afternoon. It's another "mom talent" of mine. Another talent is the ability to talk in code and understand the great riddles of what is being said.

"I'm going to fix some lunch. Are you hungry?" The real translation of my question is: "I think you have been alone with him long enough. Let's go."

"Sure, I guess I can eat." Genny's real translation is: "I can't believe you are doing this to me! I hate you!"

"I'll catch up with you later?" Genny asks Kent, but what she is really saying is: "I'm so sorry. My mom is so lame. We'll talk all about how unfair she is later."

"Yeah, sure." Kent's translation is: "This is super awkward so I am just going to sit real still and agree to whatever is said and smile. Can't forget to smile."

Kent smiles. Genny blushes. Genny glares at me as she walks past. The world keeps turning. Que Sera, Sera….

Sitting in the backseat of the car, the metal edge of the can opener seems harder to twist than normal. The added pressure of keeping what I am doing a secret is not helping the matters I am sure. I may not be able to avoid taking them back with us, but I am not FEMA. I don't have to feed the whole place.

"It smells horrible." Genny's nose wrinkles with disgust as the 'stew' slops its way into the plastic camping containers with which we use to eat.

One night left stranded in the car will make you rethink what to store in your glove box. Now, at all times, there is a flashlight, plastic compact bowls that store mini silverware from our camping days, dry socks, can opener, a map and "snacks". I try to keep the basics of first aid in there too just being me, running on my wheel.

Genny's first taste is timid, a small bite that she rolls around in her mouth before committing to a larger sample.

The gourmet dog food is not the processed can of thick, gelled substance I was fearing, but closer to the style that Ginjer used to feed Mintzy. It is chunks of meat and a blending of vegetables with a gravy sauce. I hate to admit it, but minus the smell, it really does pass as stew and most likely, better than anything I have ever tried to put together. With Genny already being accustomed to food with questionable substances, this may go over better than expected.

"If I can close my eyes, get past what it really is, it's not the worst thing I have had to eat," she says, and I love when Genny proves me right and insults me in the same breath.

"What are we going to tell Ginjer it is?" To answer her, I hold up several cans showing that I have already stripped them of their paper labels, hiding the truth of what they contain.

"Stew. We found lots of stew. If she asks why we went to the 'store'." I pause, letting the word sink into her dictionary, "we tell her it was for the water and stew."

"There is something else we need to talk about," I say, watching her as her walls come up with our earlier meeting not forgotten. She watches me, wearily waiting for the words that she is prepared to battle.

"You know we can't stay here. It isn't safe." I ease into the conversation with hopes she will at least listen to me before erupting with teen angst. "We can't take them all with us. That, too, wouldn't be safe." I stir my 'stew' avoiding her stare.

"...but Alicia?" She has dropped her voice to a whisper.

"Of course, I am going to approach Alicia. My fear is though she may already have emotional ties with them not allowing her just to leave. If she asks us to take them all, what am I supposed to do?" She understands my dilemma and nods with her eyes staring off into the math of the problem.

"What about Kent and his dad, Terrence?" She is hesitant with her question, fearing my answer and my reaction to her curiosity.

"Terrence seems to be one of the main guys here. I don't know if he would be willing to leave either. I really doubt he'd let his son leave if he is staying." I know this is not the answer she wanted, but the truth is often not what we want to hear. Her shoulders sag with the defeat of it.

She stares at me, her mind trying to keep pace, outwitting my arguments. "It would be safer with us, though. Isn't that what parents are supposed to want for their kids?"

I smile at her, a soft smile of sadness and say to her, "He doesn't know that. He doesn't know us. I would not just trust someone that says it's safe because they say so."

"You came here," she says to me, and she stuns me with her logic. I have no defense to it.

"...but I will try to talk to him, okay?" I reach out to her, hoping to instill some form of hope. Her face tells me how disappointed she is with it all with her creased forehead and sad eyes. A part of my heart breaks for her, and for a moment, I am willing to risk it all to keep her happy. "I'll figure something out," I whisper it, and I am not sure to whom I am trying to convince that I can fix this.

"No, you are right," she says to me, her voice like porcelain, thin and fragile. "It's not safe. Not only will we be risking us, but we might be risking them, too. That's not fair to any of us."

"I'll figure it out." I repeat again, this time for her and the hope of seeing a smile return to her face.

She nods with no more joy than she held before. "It's okay. We are safer in our small number. I know that. The more people there are the more risks we take. It's more supplies that we will need. The longer it takes us to mobilize if something goes wrong. There are greater risks of infections if someone gets sick. We have to think with our heads now. We can't afford the risk."

There is a moment when every parent realizes that our children are not babies anymore. Most times it is caused by a joyous event such as their first prom, the first time they pull out of the driveway in a car, when they walk across a stage in a cap and gown or for some it comes with a white dress and silk lace. Not for me. My little girl has grown up in a matter of months not because she wanted to - she was forced.

There are no more proms or stages. There are no more white gowns with bouquets of flowers grasped in nervous hands. There are just the thoughts of life and death with the risks that go along with them.

This is not the way for a sixteen-year-old to have to live, but it is. This is how we now live; alone and disjointed from the world. Friendships are weighed by the risk it involves to maintain them and the supplies it would take to nurture them. The risk I stand of losing the Genny I once knew outweighs it all.

Chapter 11

I have gone over the words a thousand times in my head. I have mentally approached it from every angle, but I can't make the words form. My mouth opens, but I stand there mute and blank like an idiot.

Genny now talks to Kent as if it is the last time she will ever see another human being. She hangs on his every word. She laughs a little too hard at his jokes. She stares at him so hard I wonder if she is trying to memorize his features or just freak the kid out. I think she is accomplishing a little bit of both with her actions.

I think I am most afraid of the fact, that when I do say the words, of how things will change for us. Right now, I don't have to face the fact that Alicia may not want to leave with me. I don't have to finally pull Genny away from Kent and watch the crushing sadness that it will cause her. In a weird twist of fate, the reason we came here may just become the reason that we have to stay.

"What-cha doing?" Alicia says with mischief, thinking she can tease me by catching me doing something naughty. "Going all Dear Diary on me?"

"Nope, just trying to keep from going insane." I smile back at her, closing the notebook of my ramblings.

"Soooo, you're telling me you are out of tequila?" We both smile at her joke.

I remember those nights of shots and bonding over the injustices of mankind. I also remember the rounds of "Truth or Dare" that it resulted in, and at our age, we really shouldn't have kept calling 'dare.'

"Yup, all out of tequila."

Half laughing with the thoughts of another time, we fall into a comfortable silence with one another.

The group, 'townsfolk' and all, sit around a low burning fire to help fight off the winter chill. The benefit of coastal living of South Carolina is the almost lack of winter. Where we are, snow is an oddity and most nights barely dip to the border of freezing. Come summer though, we will all wish we lived elsewhere.

The flames dance with each pop and crackle, casting sparks into the air that scatter before wilting away. There is a constant low murmuring as conversation flows, melding with the chirping of crickets. It is sometimes punctured with an overbearing laugh that stalls the flow of the conversations with imagined fears, straining to hear any hints of having disturbed something in the woods before the whole process starts again. Everyone glances over their shoulders into the darkness surrounding us randomly. We are like children fearing the monsters from camp stories that our minds imagine for us with vivid detail.

"How well do you know these people?" I am trying once again to build the courage to speak what is on my mind.

"How well do we know anyone, anymore? I have seen people change their whole demeanor when things start to go wrong. Sometimes, it's for the better, but most times for the worse." She stares at me, her teal-green eyes searching my face. "Why?" Her question stalls my tongue with the moment being here that I have been scared to attempt to reach.

"Just curious. I was wondering-" Before I can start my dreaded question, the conversation around us shreds into silence. The way so many are staring into one spot of the darkness, my stomach clenches before dropping into a nervous pit.

I don't know who heard what first. I am only part of the staring contest with the woods that have started. Eyes squint, trying to decipher what the sound was that someone signaled, attempting to coax knowledge out of the shadows. A few stand, thinking it will help their senses to verify if there even was a sound, but it is the silence that now surrounds us that is the best clue that something is watching us.

There is a part of us, even after all these years of compliance, which still understands the way of nature when the only division of the world was once hunter or prey. For a time, we were the hunters. Now, we are the prey and we freeze like prey, searching for a hint of the direction of our deaths.

He comes out of the darkness like a demon from a dark corner of dread. The flesh of his face is torn in long, furrowed lines as if at one point someone tried to claw his face in the fight for their survival. His clothes are stained and gaping where they have snagged, tearing themselves on objects in his path. His faded eyes stare at us with intent, roaming our gathering as one would pick the best cut of meat from a butcher. He possesses the steady calm of what they are, just watching and waiting for our first move with his arrival. When it comes, he swells with the excitement of the hunt.

The screams explode around the camp with sudden intensity, bouncing off the trees to send the sounds back ringing out in the night. It fills the woods with our panic sending birds to flight like dark silhouettes against the night sky. Strategic plans are left unanswered with the minds around us racing with fears of their deaths. It is exactly what he wanted.

With a blank face he comes straight into the group, sending them running with a divided wave to either side. Alicia and I stand in the back watching it all with wide, fear-filled eyes. Something inside me knows, this isn't right. I stand mute, watching the demon section off parts of our group. His eyes are always moving as he keeps his plan in motion. He isn't attacking. He is herding. There are more coming.

"Genny!" The group has parted, crowding the area into small sections, blocking my path to my daughter.

"Genny!" Alicia screams with me. Both of our hearts are pounding in our chests with our panic adding strength to our voices.

"Mom? Aunt Alicia?" We turn and pivot trying to pin-point her voice amid all the screams and disorientation of the running people around us with bodies bumping against us.

The screams change from the onset of his arrival. They are no longer the notes of panic, but of pain before falling into the gurgling pitches of death. Just as I had feared, the camp is now over-run with them and the help the first one gave separating us into smaller herds of prey to be fed upon made it so easy. From the same pitch-black darkness, they emerged, silent shadows of death wearing stains like badges of honor from past battles. They destroy body after body with their madness, spraying blood in high arches or letting it pour straight from the font in their suckling mouths. Either way, it is red and it coats everything around us. The air is desecrated with not only the sounds of so many deaths, but also the sharp, metallic scents.

"GENNY!" I am screaming with the strength of my soul now to find her, fearing that it might be her under claw-like hands and tearing teeth.

"Mom! Aunt Alicia!" I hear her again, and my heart soars when I finally see her. My daughter, my brave, genius daughter, is sitting in the car flashing the high beams at us with Ginjer waving frantically in the seat beside her. She did just as we have always practiced. When the shit hits the fan, you get the hell out.

My knees are weak with my body's adrenaline release when I know she is safe. Alicia half drags me, half leaves me, with our escape, forcing me to keep up with her or be left behind. All around me, screams are dispersing with the sounds of engines or the gurgles of death. Bodies lie twitching as their flesh is chewed from their limbs or torsos by who were once the true inhabitants of this town.

Wearing everything from tailored suits to cotton nightgowns, they crouch or bend over the steaming bodies, pulling the torn flesh or thicker, darker parts into starving mouths that drip with the blood from the meat upon which they are feasting. Wet, suction like noises fill the void of screams as they dine from body cavities in small groups. My stomach turns rancid from watching it and it feels as if we have been running for miles to reach the car while those fall around us only had the chance to take small steps.

"Go!" Alicia screams before she and I are firmly in the car. Genny slams the car into reverse, thrusting me sideways as I slam the door shut, attempting to seal the sounds away from us.

The headlights illuminate what was just a moment ago a peaceful night around the fire. It has turned into a banquet of mutilation. If Norman Rockwell ever painted with Alice Cooper, he would have the perfect motivation with what is before me. Some of the turned town stare at our departing cars with eyes that flash bright when the lights hit them, taking notice of which way the cars are leaving. As cruel and as damning as it is, I hope that enough have fallen to feed them well enough to forget about us.

"Where do I go? Where do I go?" Genny is near hysterical. Her voice vibrates in high pitches with her stress.

"Follow the cars." I reach around her seat to hold her the best I can, trying to ease some of her fears.

"They should all be heading to the movie theater. Just head to the theater." Alicia is watching the back of the car, fearing that at any moment we will see them following us into the night. Their eyes watching us as their bodies glow in the taillights with a demonic red tint. Their bodies covered in the still dripping gore of their murders while searching for ours.

The car is filling with our heavy breathing, panting from the run and from the emotions that fill our bodies. Alicia's mind is with those who we have lost and may have lost. Ginjer's mind is with the thoughts of how close she came to joining them. Genny is fighting to see through her tears with the visions of what we left repeating in her mind and I know she is concerned for Kent, the only friend she has had in months.

My only thoughts are of gratitude for my daughter's safety and the relief that she kept to the plan. Her first, the rest of us if possible, but always her first to escape is what we agreed on the day we had to leave the mansion. I would gladly accept my death if she stuck with the plan, thinking of herself first. I could not accept my life if I lost her to save another. I might be forced to kill the one that cost me her life, making me no better than the things we run from now. Just like them, the death I cause would be slow and painful.

There are a handful of cars in the dark parking lot. Electricity stopped long ago, leaving the tall lamps that once provided light for the lot useless and menacing with their scrolling metalwork setting a gothic feeling. They leave us only the moon's light to search for any signs of the group among the other cars parked here.

"Do you see anyone?" Ginjer leans high on the dash, peering through the windshield waiting for any small movement to spook her. Her hair glows a darker shade of orange than her normal strawberry coloring with only the moon to guide us.

"We don't normally pull up front and start waving our arms with every car we see." Alicia leans closer to the door's window staring into the darkness. "Normally we try to blend in with the other cars and wait to see what happens."

The moon is often paralleled in romantic sonnets, but when it is just the dim white light hindering the search for what may be waiting to kill you, there is nothing amorous about the situation. Searching the lot to discover a parked preschool van proves how correct I am. The white converted van is painted in bold colors with the name of the school it once serviced. All around it there are dancing clowns with their large smiles and floating balloons. The smiles may as well have held rows of pointed teeth for the way my heart skipped when passing it.

"Maybe we are at the wrong theater?" I ask with hope, unable to take my eyes from the van and what it may imply by being here.

"No, this is the one. We double-checked it on the map. It is pretty much the center of town, making it easy to get to for everyone, even if separated."

The logic behind her idea makes sense. I wish it didn't.

"Maybe they went inside? Hoping to hide just in case we were followed?" Genny is slowly running out of rows of cars and wants to believe we are not the only ones to have escaped.

"It's possible," Alicia says and then smiles. "Very possible. Look!"

We turn to see where she is pointing and spot the very southern Jeep with the large tires and its decals declaring for the South. The smile is contagious, spreading quickly through the car. We know at least one other set made it out alive. We just have to find them.

"Guess Lover Boy is tougher than we thought." My smile is mockingly returned to me by Genny from the rearview mirror. She turns her face from me before the genuine smile pulls on her lips.

"Lucky us…" Ginjer mutters, earning her looks from the other two women in the car.

"Park the car and let's find them." I instruct Genny before more comments can be made.

Her apprehension for breaking what was once a basic law stalls her mind for a fraction of time. "…but this is handicapped?" She blushes and blurts out, "Never mind," she quickly tries to counter, before the teasing can begin. She wasn't fast enough to avoid the snickering, though.

We ease out of the car with the grace of one being stalked. We each cringe with the sound of the doors closing. The still lot allows for every sound to be intensified, amping-up our nerves to new heights. We glance in every direction as we make our way to the tall cement building plastered with posters peeking out from grime-covered glass. Behind the thick layers of neglect, their colors are faded, as almost everything is now. I wouldn't mind having a few of the weapons the actors are posed with before entering the place.

The doors show no sign of any entrance in a long time. Trash is piled in the crevice the doors create between the two ticket booths. There is no wide sweeping of an arch or even a disturbed path showing any movements from the doors. The glass here is just as thick with grimy film as the glass encasing the posters, preventing anyone from seeing what inside might hold with such dim light from the moon. I don't see any spots of swiped glass to mimic a cleaning motion by someone who was here, either. If they are here, how did they get in? Did they even stop to check to see what could be waiting for us inside?

Ginjer rattles the doors with the metal bars and the firm lock holds them in place. The trace of dirt left on her hands repeating the proof that no one has come this way in some time. With one highly arched eyebrow she looks to Alicia silently asking *Now what?*

"A door around back?" Genny still clings to the hope of what the Jeep means, refusing to walk away so easily.

"Can't hurt to look?" Alicia shrugs, leading the way around the building to where the moon is even less giving of its light.

I follow last, trusting myself to the job of keeping eyes out for things that go bump in the night. As I stare into the parking lot, the van once again leaps into my vision. The painted clowns seem to be grinning with hidden mischief. Their faces mimicking my sister's comment, turning it into something more than what she had originally meant.

"Can't hurt to look?" They ask me in my mind with their cocked heads and black painted eyes peering around the cars parked around them.

"Can't hurt to look?" They repeat, and this time the secret that they are keeping flutters in my chest before clawing at my stomach.

Chapter 12

We did find a door on the side of the stone building that had been pried open. The pile of decaying trash left dark outlines on the cement from where it had stood for so long. The door wails on dry hinges as we open it, setting a mental rush of fears playing in our minds at what we may have alerted to our presence.

We enter into one of the many theaters. Row after row of seats are resting empty, tilting upward with the floor. The air is stagnant, suffocating after being confined for so long. We fight against the coughing of our lungs caused by the disturbed dust that swirls with each step.

Our little train stops at the door that adjoins this room with what I imagine to be a long hallway with access to each theater and the main lobby. When no sounds stir, Alicia pushes the door open slowly, preparing to slam it closed with the first hint of any danger.

She and Ginjer exit into the hall first, with an eager Genny following them. With one last glance over my shoulder, I leave the theater behind me with the cobwebs blowing in the high corners from the wind entering with the door left opened. I wrestle with the idea of rushing over to close it, but if others truly are trying to find us, it may provide them with a hint as to where we are. I just pray it doesn't provide anything else that may be looking for us with a hint.

Please Lord, don't let my daughter see me die today.

The hall is a long cavern of shadows. There are no windows to provide slivers of light, and once the door closes behind me, the darkness becomes alive. My skin crawls with the sensations of spiders' feet feeling the shadows watching me. The rush of adrenaline makes my scalp tingle with apprehension. Every snap or pop I imagine is something jumping from the unseen darkness to overtake me.

Please Lord, don't let my daughter see me die today.

The stillness is so encompassing that I can hear the pounding of my heart. It fills my ears with its beating like a drum song of dread. The sharp beats are short and forceful like a march to an execution, telling those who gather near about the event that is about to happen. It's pounding with such a force I fear for the damage it might do to my ribs with its pulsing.

Please Lord, don't let my daughter see me die today.

The hall appears to be growing, mimicking every movie I have ever seen. I wait for each door that we pass to sway open, showing me the dark secrets I fear they might contain. The once beloved actors' eyes seem to follow our progress. The grime is presenting illusions on their faces, contorting with silent pleas for us to turn around. As I see what is lying in the next doorway, I wish we had listened.

Please Lord, don't let my daughter see me die today.

The hall is laid with a vivid carpet, setting the stage for the feeling of attending red carpet premieres of the movies that once played here. In the darkness, the red is a muted burgundy with the dust hiding the true glory the carpet once held. Ahead of us, the carpet's coloring is spotted even darker, like a stain besmirching its honor. It is dotted in an irregular pattern that weaves side to side, but always forward. Our eyes follow it, never glancing higher than the point of the trail right before us. We walk around it, fearing the stain will cling to us like a sin. Like a crack to a mother's back, we tip-toe around the damnation in fear of stepping on it.

Please Lord, don't let my daughter see me die today.

The once small, splattering of freckles now grows larger and more numerous. We can no longer avoid them without moving fully around portions of the hall. When one of us does step on one, the carpet is stiff and crunches under their feet. In a place of such silence, it sounds as loud as brittle bones breaking. The pattern dissolves into a dried pool like pattern of stained, dark black crimson that slides under the doorway beside us with one giant long smear. The three of us silently stare at the half-hidden message of what has happened here. Our nightmares are not lacking in numbers already and since the blood is old, dried from the sins committed in the past, we silently agree to let the secrets rest undisturbed. It feels almost heartless to let whatever sleeping secret lies to further decay alone in the dark, but what comfort can we offer the dead?

A flash of light, so sudden and shocking it startles us comes from the lobby ahead. Without thought, I clamp my hand over Genny's mouth to suffocate a scream. Standing in the pool of dried blood flickers my mind to a sense of foreshadowing while watching the beam of light that comes and goes.

"What is the plan?" I whisper into her ear, making her startle with finally hearing a true sound.

"Get out. Don't look back. Use the notebooks. Brain first, heart second." Genny whispers the rehearsed words against my palm. We have repeated them like prayers at night.

"Can you two not plan for funerals just yet?" Ginjer hisses from a shadow across from us.

"Who has time for funerals?" Alicia slides along the wall, leaving a smudge against the posters where her body traveled.

Ginjer copies each step Alicia makes, keeping perfect pace with her. It strikes me how far the pampered socialite has come from the days of chilled wine on poolside patios to facing the dangers that lurk at every corner, forcing her fears at bay. I wonder what this world holds for my daughter and how it will form her.

No longer risking Genny going first, I pull her behind me, shielding her with my body from whatever is waiting in the lobby. The light has stopped with our whispering, marking it as manual and not as a result from something from nature. Something with intelligence is holding its breath as we creep forward. The only question is, why did it signal at all?

Please Lord, don't let my daughter see me die today.

Signaling for Ginjer to drop out of sight, Alicia crouches to the floor at the corner of the hall. She pulls from a pocket of her jeans a small compact mirror and holding her breath she extends her hand out, tilting the mirror to see what may be hiding from us. Slowly, she pans the room with as far as the mirror will allow her borrowed sight to see. She shakes her head, telling us she doesn't see anything, but it doesn't erase our fears.

When the beam comes rapidly again, instantly we shrink back against the wall, slapping it with our bodies in our haste to hide. Genny melts down the length of the wall and I follow her movement, becoming one of the many dark shadows of the hall.

"It's Morse code." Genny's whisper turns our heads back to where we last saw the beam.

Alicia makes a sound of amusement watching the rapid pulses of the beam become a set of patterns.

.... . .-.. .-.. ---   .... . .-.. .-.. ---   .... . .-.. .-.. ---

The beam flashes against the wall of the lobby, pausing before repeating the pattern again and again. Genny's face wrinkles with her concentration level, trying to remember the small lesson held in a long gone class.

"I'm not positive, but I think it says, 'hills'." Genny is confused by what the word would be used for in a dark lobby.

"It says, 'hello'." Ginjer doesn't turn to us when she corrects the word. She stares out into the void, but feels our eyes just the same. "My husband was a pilot." She does her normal shrug of non-importance about sharing the fact of her life.

"Now what?" I ask the women who have decided to become the leaders of our little band.

Alicia was never one for debates or long talks about choices made in life and their outcomes. She hasn't changed. Without a hint to her plan, she stands and walks into the lobby as steady as if she owned the room and calls back what the code was flashing.

"Hello?" After whispering for so long, her call is as loud as a scream of suffering. "Terrence?"

If I had thought of the place as a tomb before, now as we strain to hear the smallest sound it feels like time has stopped, stealing the air and noise from the building. A shuffling comes from the center of the lobby where once perky teens would have stood offering over-priced popcorn with their syrup drinks and enough items to satisfy the sugar rush of the last minute impulse buy. Panic invades our minds, flashing pictures of what may possibly be hiding from us. Panic never pictures butterflies, kittens, or even loppy-eared puppies. Panic watches too many horror movies, also.

"Alicia?" The voice is as tentative as a kid meeting Santa for the first time wondering if he is real and if he is really here?

Genny is the first to recognize the voice and my arms are not strong enough to keep her in the hall any longer. "Kent?" she calls out into the darkness.

Large eyes stare out at us from between the boxes of forgotten candy in the glass cases. His lingering doubts prove that I am not the only parent that drills their children with the importance of the safety that is needed to survive. His goofy teen smile spreads across his face at the sight of Genny. It clenches my stomach more now than it would have if I were simply watching my daughter and her date months back. All that was at risk then were days of moping when they broke up. Now, there might be years of it when I forcefully pull them apart.

They hug over the glass case, forgetting the many eyes of adults that are on them before embarrassment makes them clumsy.

"Touching, but where are the rest?" Ginjer is not amused by the reunion. She has never shown a lot of patience for the boy. I just can't place why. The woman who made a living from being married seems to have a low opinion for dating.

"Dad, Collin and Peyton went looking to make sure the place was secure. Just in case, we had to hold up here and wait stuff out. They went down the other hallway." Kent points down another long hall that might as well have been a mouth to a cave with the darkness leering from it.

"Anyone else make it?" Alicia is counting the death toll in her head. A very real fact that one night might have reduced us to only a handful.

"Not yet," he tells her, as sadness holds hands with hope in his voice. "We didn't even think y'all made it out, but here you are…" his voice trails off, leaving the meaning of his thoughts between us. He's right. There may still be more.

My sister leans against the glass case, holding her head to hands pressing firmly together. Her dark brown hair enfolds her face, preventing me from seeing her expression. If she is praying or just exhausted, it is hard to tell, but I hope God is taking notice either way.

"How long have they been gone?"

I watch as Kent tries to figure out the math of my question. Watching him makes me wish the popcorn machines were still functioning. It is almost a small comedy in itself.

"They left way before I heard y'all. I haven't heard anything since and I heard a lot of noise from your group. I mean, a lot, of noise." He smirks, amused by his interpretation of our blundering entrance. The way Alicia and Ginjer are staring at him, I smirk too, but for a different reason. Once again, I wish for the popcorn machine.

"Why were you flashing the light, Genius?" Ginjer is not accustomed to having someone mock her. At least, in her old circle, they had the grace to do it behind each others' back.

"It's what Dad told me to do if I think I know who is coming in. It's a way to get their attention without making any noise to attract the other things." His look of confusion over what he has done wrong is genuine. Just as genuine as the look Ginjer gives me about him.

Alicia sighs, the events have begun to take its toll on all of us. "Light attracts them too, Kent." Her statement fills him again with confusion and she chooses to skip right over it. "We need to figure out where Peyton, Collin, and Terrence are. If anyone else was coming, we would have seen them by now."

It hurts her to have to admit the truth. So far, most of their former group is either missing or dead and the night is not over yet. The death toll can still rise.

Alicia slowly becomes the leader Kent knows her as and he responds to the authority of her voice. "Have you seen anything else in this place?"

"No. Just us when we got here. Then y'all and nothing else." Kent glances around him, hoping nothing is stalking the shadows waiting to prove him wrong.

I keep my peace about the nagging sensation that claws at me. I have been looking at the lobby while they held their conversations with nothing to add to it myself. There are subtle hints all over the room that something happened here whispering to me shy warnings. The fake potted trees by the entrance are leaning, pushed from a panicked exit. They now rest, supported by the same colored velvet ropes as the carpet. Once used to usher the flow of traffic into the place, the ropes no longerline up, but are askew making a disjointed path. It gives the appearance of a traffic rush either in or out of the room from the last real crowd that was here.

Cups and paper buckets advertising the latest block-buster are strewn across the floor in strategic places from the opposite concession stand. They almost appear to have been thrown at something, or someone, that stood across from them. Looters would not have gone through the efforts to land them in the same general area. The trash would be everywhere or left alone.

On the walls, there are random streaks of darker grime with jagged edges of different lengths. Oval stains with long paths pulled from them spot the lobby floor that holds the décor of a once well-maintained place. Stains such as these are not something the owner would have let slip by his or her attention. So, if they weren't there when the theater was in operation, then when, and by what were they made?

Where are the owners from the cars left sitting in the lot? The caked dirt tells the passage of time they have sat here alone and forgotten. The clowns peer at me through the other cars' windows. Their colors don't seem as bright and cheery as they were when I first saw them, but their smiles are still just as unsettling. Where are the children?

I think I will stay here with the kids," I offer, still staring at the clowns and fearing what their presence may mean.

Alicia and Ginjer follow my stare and both inhale with the discovery.

"You don't think..." Ginjer stalls, letting her silence fill in for the words no one wants to assume.

If you were running away from something with that many kids, wouldn't you get back in the van if it were possible?" Alicia is just the bearer of evil truths tonight.

Genny whispers, "So, they are still here?" holding tighter to Kent's hand.

e each look to the other, feeling discomfort from the thoughts we are having. Some thoughts are just too horrible to endure. *Forgive me Father for my sins, but I pray that if they are still here, we find them dead. Truly dead.* My thoughts betray my bravery.

I have had to kill my fair share of things to survive, but I don't know if I could bring myself to do the same to children no matter what they might be now.

Genny looks to me for guidance in this new storm, but I have no idea where port is any longer. I just know that it feels like we are sinking more each day into an abyss from which I don't see an escape. The current grows stronger with each new struggle, pulling us further from the shore of who we once were and I don't know if we are strong enough to ever swim back.

"Can't hurt to look?" Was the question that was asked of us when we arrived. Right now, it could hurt a lot. It could even destroy us.

Chapter 13

The three of us sit behind the glass cage, waiting for the return of the rest of our new group. Every noise steals our breath, making our hearts race and our bodies freeze with dread. The buzzing of the occasional fly even sets our hearts to race. The tension wears thin the slim hopes of conversation and soon we sit in silence laced with facial expressions of doubt.

How long do you think they have been gone?" Kent's emotions are a mask on his face. He wears every thought and every feeling, making him an easy person to understand and to tease.

"Don't know. Why don't you check your phone for the time?" Genny's off-flavored comment arches my eyebrow at her. The saint isn't normally snippy. "Sorry, just tired. I'm sure it feels a lot longer than it actually has been." She smiles at Kent, expressing her remorse for the comment. He smiles, just that easy to appease. The river doesn't run deep with this boy.

Genny rattles the left over gummy bears in her looted box of candy. "What do you think the expiration date is on these things?"

"Wouldn't it have been smart to check that before you started eating them?" Kent stares at her, watching her eyebrows knit as her mind is searching for a response. "Sorry, just tired. I'm sure they taste like they have sat there a lot longer than they actually have been." He smiles at her, the pride he is feeling over his wit lighting his eyes. The blow Genny lands on his arm dims it some.

"You're going to let him talk to me like that?" She tries to mock a pout with pursed lips and sad eyes, but fails. Her giggles are a give away to her mischief.

I shrug and tell her, "He has a point," finishing off the rest of my looted boxed chocolate. "Good thing I didn't encourage you to steal milk. Who knows how that might have ended."

Our teasing chatter covered the sounds of their return. So when Alicia, seeing the perfect chance to be an annoying big sister, reaches over the glass to grab my shoulders, Genny and I both scream. Kent jumps so hard backwards at our distress that the perfectly balanced paper tubs came crashing down on him. He kicks at them as if he is under attack, sending them flying even higher in the air before crashing down on him again. The sight must have been hilarious by the laughter that follows. The three of us on this side of the case aren't laughing at all.

"You suck," is the only response I can think of with my heart choking me. I obviously missed my mark because Alicia just laughs even harder.

"How many buckets of popcorn did you want, Son?" Terrence leans nonchalantly on the case, staring down at his panting teen. His face is all mirth, but Kent is not amused.

"Well did you at least find anything?" Genny stands, ready to confront them before anyone can tease her.

"Yes, we did." Peyton is carrying a large cardboard box. His smile is just as proportionate.

"It looks like this place has never been disturbed. We found no trace of looting damage. Nothing has been broken into. There is food, even if it is candy, still just sitting here. The best? These..." Peyton's smile grows even larger as he opens the box.

He pulls out large, rolled fabric, tossing them on the floor. They are held together with strings tied to keep them rolled. The material is reflective even with this meager light. Personally, I still think the candy is the best, but these are a nice comfort, too.

"Sleeping bags?" Genny tilts her head as if it is a game of charades and the first clue has been tossed in front of her.

"Yup, sleeping bags, Kiddo. This place must have once held some kind of overnight thing or maybe movies on the lawn. Whatever it was, they left these up in the storage area," Alicia says as she rubs Genny's head and earns herself a glare. Someone is still in trouble.

Ginjer and I exchange glances, once again I feel the shame creep over me. I have been thinking of how rough we have had it living as we live, but seeing them this excited over sleeping bags only proves how wrong I have been. We have been taking for granted the simple things that could mean a completely new level of comfort to some.

"We planning to stay here tonight?" Ginjer steals the timing for any comment I may have been building, preventing me from telling them the truth about us.

"We might as well," Terrence shrugs. "Don't really want to be looking for a new place to set up in the dark."

"…and others may still show up." Peyton stares out into the parking lot with hope. His eyes float over the cars, trying to see if he spots anything familiar. His posture is one of defeat thinking of all of the people he wasn't able to save. Seeing their leader saddened, it sweeps over the room like a silent prayer.

"They wouldn't let me bring down the Johnny Depp poster," Ginjer mutters, rolling out her bag completely impervious to the mood of the room. "What?" she asks, staring back at the shocked faces towards her. "It's not like it's going to any good use just sitting up there!"

The adults stare at her, half hiding our smirks, wondering if she even is aware of the corner, she has backed herself into with that comment. No one is brave enough really to ask with the social lines still blurring with our two groups. When Genny opens her mouth, I step on her foot warning her not to open that conversation.

With no safe avenue left for conversation to travel along, we begin prepping for sleep. Peyton agrees to take the first shift to watch for anyone else who might arrive. They assure me the door in the back that I left open has been shut and for extra measure, they have wedged a metal bat the theater used as a promotional prop in the handles of that theater's hallway entrance.

"We are all safe and secure." Peyton smiles at me and I feel myself returning it before I can counter the emotion. Worse, not before Genny can see it.

"Totally saw that." She is munching on another box of candy and for a brief moment, I have an urge to tell her no more candy before bedtime. Some habits are hard to break.

"He is a good looking guy," I say to her, because there is no point in arguing with her or trying to deny my smile. Instead, I stare at the man whose back is to us as he leans against the glass doors searching for some signs of hope about the ones we left behind.

"How long has it been since you dated?" Her calm question spins my head to her. "Mom, I'm sixteen. I totally know what sex is." She is making a game of tossing the bears into the air and catching them with her mouth. Glad to see I am the only one uncomfortable here.

"Genny, you're sixteen. I totally want to deny that you know what sex is." She makes a 'tsking' noise at my comment between bites.

"You know, that is how most teen pregnancies happen. Parents just don't feel comfortable talking to us about sex. Then we have to go online, gather our own information –" I hold my hand up to stop her rant, blocking the line of thought before my sanity becomes as torn and mangled as the candy bears she is eating.

"At what point did you decide to make this conversation the most uncomfortable that you could?" I ask, and she smiles at me and I have to return it. This is the Genny that I have been missing.

"When I saw you smile." She sits up, looking at me. All the impish grins are set aside. "I'm not saying you have to marry the guy, or even love him. You don't know what tomorrow might bring and if we are all going to die anyway, you might as well get a little something while you can."

The sincere mixture of her words and emotions disturbs me a little. I never thought that I would be receiving "go get 'em" advice from my teen daughter.

"Hey Genny," I look at her, my face a blank slate of unwritten words. "Why don't you pull your stuff a little closer to me? Suddenly, I don't feel as giving as I was with your alone time with Kent."

"Mom," she laughs, as we begin a game of assault with the gummy bears she was eating, tossing them back and forth. "You don't have to worry about me. I have seen enough movies to know the virgin outlives everyone and the stupid teen girl who is talked into sex is always the first to die."

"Who is the first to die?" Ginjer comes to our area hearing our laughter. She and I are still keeping apart from the other group. Watching my sister and Terrence talk over the night's plans for our safety, I am stabbed with guilt and jealousy simultaneously.

"Sluts," Genny offers shrugging causally. I don't want to have to explain the previous conversation, but her response only leaves me less wiggle room to get out of having to.

"How did you know the word was, 'hello'?" Ginjer enjoys talking about herself. I throw her the conversation and hope to silently sneak away before I can become the main topic.

"Told you, my husband was a pilot. You know that." She shuts down, staring out into the lobby that we have made into a giant bedroom.

"He taught you Morse code?" Genny asks innocently, unaware of Ginjer's unusual silence.

"No, his slut did." Her smile is like candy-coated arsenic. It seems sweet at first, but the words behind it scald with poison. "He was having an affair with a stewardess. They would send texts in Morse code thinking they were clever just in case I ever saw the phone before he could delete the text. He told me they were running practice tests so they could both pass any random skill testing, with a smile and a pat on my head." Her smile becomes less sweet, but still filled with venom. "So, I began jotting down the dashes and such and translating them through search engines. It didn't take long to figure out what was going on once their magical code was broken. So, I waited for him to take a trip and sent him a text in my own code."

Genny is so eager to hear the rest, she almost jumps up when Ginjer stops the story before she begins again.

"I sent him two numbers, the longitude and latitude of where I left his precious sports car. When he came home a day later than normal, mad that all he found was the empty parking lot to a very expensive jewelry store, I simply smiled at him. "Isn't texting in codes fun?" I asked him. "Turns out, my lawyer knows Morse code very well and figured up exactly what it would cost you in alimony should a judge ever learn Morse code, too." After that little bomb he was much more discreet if he ever cheated again and I had a very pretty diamond ring to wear every time I thought he was."

"Why didn't you just divorce him?" It is a question I have wanted to ask since I began working for her, being well aware of their internal issues and now finally I have.

"When you divorce, your issues become public. That's just messy for everyone." Her voice is almost judgmental with me being a divorcee myself and I shrug, ignoring the tone she has directed at me. I gave up a long time ago trying to please a woman whose idea of 'budgeting' was only buying five new outfits a day instead of her normal twelve.

I refuse to become insulted by her and begin to settle into "bed", proving to her that the conversation is over. After a few minutes of silence, Ginjer goes back to her bag that she has placed closer to us than the others with nothing more being said between us.

"You know she doesn't really mean the things she says, Mom?" Genny's whisper caresses my mind that has slowly begun to shut down from the day.

"I know." I pat her leg, letting her know that I am not really upset.

"Do you think Dad and Kim are out there, somewhere? We found Aunt Alicia," her voice is fragile, fearing the truth.

I lie, trying to give a glimmer of hope to her dreams so I tell her, "I don't know. I guess they could be."

When she closes her eyes, I hope she is seeing him as he was and not as I last saw him. I hope he is smiling at her, sharing jokes that only they knew with their private father/daughter relationship. I hope she is dreaming of what it would be like to find him, whole and safe, hugging him for that first time after so many months apart. I hope she cherishes that dream, and I will lie about it forever to avoid tarnishing her memory of him.

For me, I know the truth. I can still see him hunched over his new wife, tearing her apart with no remorse or recognition for her. I can still remember Kim's vacant, staring eyes pointed at me with her arm extended in her death as she tried to crawl away from the man that was supposed to protect and honor her. Thanks to Charlie, I will forever hear the sound that a heart makes when it is being sucked on like a rare fruit; ripe and overflowing its juices down your arm. He also taught me how to kill that day and for that, I am thankful.

Chapter 14

A feather flirts with my face. The gentle tip travels along my cheek before trailing to my neck only to repeat the pattern. It sways back and forth over me, gently waking me. A hand tugs on my arm, trying to roll me over. The playful feather is a sharp contrast to the forceful hand whose fingers are starting to bruise my flesh. The feeling switches from seduction to something different, startling my mind to a faster pace of consciousness. When Genny screams, the last fog of sleep slips away and the smell hits me, bringing me wide-awake.

My eyes open to stare into the terror-filled set across from me. Genny is staring at something behind me, mute and frozen with what she is seeing. Her body shakes so hard that the material of the sleeping bag crackles like static with the vibrations.

My eyes roll to my side and meet the faded, glazed eyes of a little girl. Her once light brown hair is now matted, making the shade darker at the tangled ends. Her face is blank as if she was startled by the scream. Her eyes are searching my face for the next outburst without any emotion of her own. Those tiny fingers are firmly applying more pressure to my arm. It feels as though she is trying to peel the flesh from my bones. My skin screams under the pain and I'm afraid to call out for help, fearing what it may trigger her to do.

We are at an impasse. She seems to be waiting for me to react and I am waiting for the flesh to be shredded from my arm. My mind is shutting down as I stare at this little girl. It is pouring itself into a tight, locked box knowing what is about to happen, not only to me, but also to what I may have to do to her.

The face that once smiled and was the pride of her parents is dried and crusted from things my mind doesn't want to acknowledge. There is a perfect, clean pattern from where her tongue had licked it away when it was still fresh as if it were the remains of a messy dessert that once coated her face. I can remember Genny doing that at this girl's age and I groan in my mind with the comparison.

Her school uniform with its blue and green plaid has dark markings on her chest. It extends wide, almost from shoulder to shoulder and the paper name tag she wears for what was supposed to have been a fun field trip reads the name "Becky" in the unsteady script of small children.

I imagine the stain to be where her victim's blood pooled while she was eating, soaking her with her sin. The white collar of her undershirt is spotted with more stains, destroying the innocence she once held with the brutal honesty of what she is now. This little girl, that one sat in a room filling papers with crayon creations is a murderer. Her tiny fingers no longer spread the colors of pastel paints, but the blood of her victims.

She smiles at me when we both feel the warmth of my blood begin to glide down my arm. It drips to the cloth of my shirt like a steady tapping finger waiting for my next move. It is waiting for me to save myself. It is *hoping* that I will save myself.

"Mom?" Genny's voice snaps the child's head in her direction.

The child, Becky, tilts her head to one side with an unnatural slow grace. Her matted hair no longer the cascading waves of what it was, sticks to the side of her raised face, falling forward to frame just her eyes. The eyes that no longer see with the child-like wonder of the world, but with the hunger of an animal that can't be abated.

All around us, the group is beginning to stir. Becky's eyes roam the room from her tilted position, seeing the others for the first time, but she doesn't show any emotion if her mistake startles her. She is still, just her eyes moving from one bag to the next plotting and planning in the way these things do. When her eyes fall to me, I know she has put the pattern of our deaths together in her mind, and mine is first.

She stares mutely at me with a face still plump from that chubbiness of youth. She can't be more than four and it fills me with pity for what has happened to her and for what I know I am going to have to do to save myself and my daughter from her. Her fingers no longer press into my flesh. Her emotions are withdrawn, shielded behind the lack of empathy she now carries for those around her. She is still the perfect hunter and she proved this by luring me into her trap.

She knew quickly that she was outnumbered. Even with her strength from the lack of feelings in her body, she would not be able to overtake us all. Attacking me quickly would cause noise, further alerting those she fears with her kill and survival motives. She doesn't fear death the way we do. She only fears not being able to achieve her kill and then survive for the next. When you can't feel pain, you don't fear death. She just craves the deaths of others.

The killer in her knew I was not a threat to her. I am not the type of prey that fights without being motivated. I'm a runner and I have proved it to her by sitting here this whole time waiting on her next move. She further lowered my defense by lowering her attack. Almost presenting a sense of unease or weariness to me with diabolical designs, but now that she has me where she wanted, she shows her true form.

There was not a sliver of hesitation with her attack. I have relaxed my body, making it pliable to force and she uses that to her advantage. With a calculated pattern, she yanks my arm down, forcing my body flat while allowing her to straddle me with one smooth act. It is so sudden that I am confused by the rapid shift of her mood and at a loss against her strength. She smiles in her small victory, thinking the battle is already won.

She made one mistake when she picked me to attack first, though. Something she couldn't possibly understand being void of her soul and lost to her memories of humanity. I am a mother. I will fight if I have to.

Her entire upper body leans in for the attack. Her arms shoot forward, aiming her hands for my shoulders with hopes of further pinning me down. Those same sharp baby fingers with torn nails that pressed into my arms now pierce my neck like talons, locking us together. She flexes them like a needle seeking a vein, looking for a way critically to wound me. She knows she must find a way to kill me before others can come to my rescue. Since she lacks the strength to break my neck, she is trying to bleed me out.

Her face is close to mine, trying to intimidate me so I will fear her, preventing me from fully fighting back. Her hair hangs around us like a dingy, velvet curtain blocking the sight of us from the others. Hunched over like this, she is keeping a low profile, better hiding her from untrained, sleep-filled eyes. She has planned my murder in her mind but in my mind, I'm still planning my life.

I let go of my fears and thoughts, letting myself sink to the same level of animalistic behavior as her. My fingers sink into her hair on the back of her head, the knots providing me with the perfect grip. I can feel small things crawling up my hand from her scalp. It almost steals my nerve with the roll of my stomach, but her fingers dig deeper and the pain snaps my mind back to focus. Anchoring my fingers, I tug her backwards and scream with the lightening hot pain of her talon-like fingers raking my flesh. My vision blurs from it, ebbing my strength to pull her off me.

Still latched to her hair, she fights against me to turn her head. It sends more of the things crawling along my arm with their escape from her efforts to free herself. I can feel their tiny bodies inching up me with what could be confused with a tickling sensation if I wasn't aware of what they are. Maggots from her rotting flesh are being scattered around me, and on me, invading my mind with further proof of the nightmare "Becky" has become.

She begins to pull against my hand, letting me tear the hair from her head. It's not just her hair that is giving away with her strength. The sick sound of her flesh separating from her skull rolls my stomach again.

Something thicker than blood washes the maggots away as she mutilates herself to be free from my grasp.

The demon child still sits on me. Her arms outstretched to me with her hands hooked like claws slashing the air trying to reach me. Slowly, she is sitting back up as her scalp shreds and I scream. I scream with each punch I land into her face that refuses to stay down. I scream with each punch that breaks bones into fragments in her baby-shaped face. I scream with each punch that knocks her head back with the dark, thick bloody ruin it becomes. I scream as Peyton finishes the job with one life ending thrust of his knife into her same ruined face.

Collin hauls Becky's limp corpse away, freeing me. Tremors start in my chest and radiate outwards, enslaving my body. I have no control as I shake, gasping for air. Peyton pulls me to him, rocking me, helping me collect myself. He whispers, assuring me that I'm okay. He tells me, "You're safe now. It is over." I watch a stray maggot climb the leg of my jeans whispering that it is not over. It will never be over until the maggots are claiming me, too.

I look over to see Genny sobbing in the arms of Alicia. Somewhere in the fight Alicia arrived, pulling Genny far from me and to safety. She nods at me, her tears streaking her face, letting me know that she has my daughter and that I can focus on collecting my sanity. Already the layers of calmness start to enfold me just knowing that Genny is safe.

"Looks like you need a nurse." Ginjer cringes, shuddering as she wipes away the tiny parasites from my body. "How was it even able to get this close? What if it had just attacked instead of stalling, for whatever reason that it did?" Ginjer looks to the man that holds me with her questions. She places every fault of the failure at the feet of a man that is supposed to be ensuring the security of our lives, if it is fair or not.

Terrence is shy with shame over failing us. He says, "It's my fault. I must have dozed off. It was my watch." His whisper fractures, too heavy to support his guilt. "I'm sorry."

Some of Ginjer's anger evaporates with Terrence's contrition. Alicia's just burns brighter.

"What if it had been Genny? Or Kent?" Alicia hurls her voice at him. Her emotions are choking her and she is seeking a release. "What apology would you give standing over your son's grave?"

We all flinch, feeling the pain of her question, but I know she is just getting started. Collin knows it, too. He kneels down in front her with a face filling with worry. With her still clinging to Genny, he begins whispering his version of soothing words to them both. He hopes to stall the growing storm of Alicia's anger before the full force of it lands, crashing around us and doing damage that we might not be able to repair.

Some damage is already done, leaving Terrence broken with the vision she has planted in his mind. He sits against the glass doors, head balanced on arms resting on his knees. Alicia's comment may have been out of line, but the truth of it is heavy on his conscience.

Ginjer examines the wounds on my neck with a bored expression. She stretches the skin, encouraging fresh blood to seep, letting it flow adding more layers to the already drying streaks. She does the same with the half-moon marks on my arms.

"Do you think they will get infected?" I ask the question that has become a top fear with any wounds now that medical facilities are stripped or rare to find.

"No, I am sure she washed her hands after the last person she ate." If Ginjer had smiled with the comment, I am sure I might have praised her for her off sense of humor, but the same bored expression adds a sting to her words.

"Your bedside manner sucks." I tell her and she does smile.

The humor is short lived, ending abruptly with Genny's scream. The smell of my blood in the air was like blood in the water to a shark. My screams were the ringing of a dinner bell. I called them all to the table and they stand, staring at us waiting for their meal. After all, a van doesn't carry just one child.

Chapter 15

They stand staring at us. Their faces are slack, showing no response with us spotting them. Their eyes move together with brains that possess no original thoughts or personality. They are bound together by the craving of our flesh and they work better together now in death than they ever did when they were alive.

The girls are dressed similar to how Becky was. The plaid jumpers over their white shirts of different sleeve lengths and wide, white collars are shaded with stains. The shine on their black, patent leather Mary-Jane style shoes is dulled with white scuffs marring their once perfection. Their tender flesh is disfigured from the damage that was either done to them or from the deaths they have caused. It is torn, some with wide strips of skin missing, from their limbs that ooze black liquid thicker than any blood I have ever seen. In the sheen, I can see the parasites squirming around within these gashes reflecting the dim light with their bodies.

The randomly placed boys are not any better for the senses. They wear shredded and torn dark navy slacks that show the abuse their bodies have endured. Their white collared shirts are an array of shades with each merging with the other in irregular patterns; a tie-dye effect of murders and mayhem. Together they are a collection of horrific mannequins, still and lifeless.

"Peyton," Alicia hisses her whisper. She is sliding backwards, towing Genny with her, trying to place the most distance between them and those standing at the entrance of the hallway. Their eyes roll to her in unison and it is unnerving.

Peyton knows we are all waiting for some guidance or a plan of action from him. I can feel the tightness in his arms around me as a compilation of strategies runs through him. We are poorly equipped for this with no real weapons but a few bats and one handgun. When we ran from the camp, taking the time to load the supplies was not high on the survival list and no one thought to bring in anything useful from the two vehicles that we have here. We were so eager to find each other that we forgot how dangerous things are   now. This oversight might just cost us our lives.

Peyton glances to Terrence and they share a silent agreement. When Terrence stands, it pulls the children's attention from Alicia and Genny. Their faces show the first signs of anger, seeing his movement as a signal for something starting. Collin stands, yanking their heads back to our side of the room, the tension building in their small bodies brings the monsters they are closer to the surface. Peyton gives me a tight squeeze as he is the last of the men in the room to stand. The standing men have their full attention now and their full hatred filled with carnal desires.

With their first step towards us, Collin times a perfect kick to the body of fallen Becky, sending it rolling to them. All motion halts in whatever was their last movement they took. They become statues; pale flesh and blank eyes staring at the object on the ground in front of them. Their minds rush through the possible information it contains trying to solve the riddle of what it is and why it should matter to them. Peyton was hoping for their hesitation and now he has it.

"Move." His hand comes down to grasp mine to help me stand. My legs are still shaky and I feel as if I am walking on plough mud. Each foot seems to sink deeper than it needs to find footing.

Ginjer and I walk backwards slowly, hoping our silent steps will go unnoticed by their locked minds. Alicia and my daughter fill the spot behind us with Collin and Peyton filling the area in front of us. Kent is waiting by Terrence for us to reach them with our parade of escape.

The smallest of the girls hisses. Her mind has reached the conclusion of what lays before them. Like a wave, the knowledge ripples outwards from her, spinning their heads towards us. Their anger spills forth in howls of rage and animates them with demonic desires.

"Go!" Peyton turns, shoving us around, no longer trying to sneak away.

Terrence has already unbolted the locks on the double doors. They stand wide and wait for us to run through. We don't have the weapons to stop them, but they no longer run fast. Their bodies don't have the same degree of control any longer with their tendons and tissues degenerating with decay at this stage of their life span. Only in the beginning were they able to keep up. Now most are clumsy, but still just as determined and just as deadly if they catch you.

Collin tosses Terrence one of the long velvet ropes as we rush through. With Peyton pressing against the doors to hold them closed, Terrence weaves the rope through the handles before knotting it and turns to run again. As secure as the rope looks, no one is willing to sit and test the theory.

Peyton and Collin lift Kent from either side to add speed to their escape. Alicia, Genny, Ginjer and I never pause on the path to our car. Genny tosses the keys to Alicia over the roof of the car and we all pile in, slamming the doors with an urgency to leave. The Jeep has already begun pulling out of the lot. The large tires are abusing the asphalt with its haste.

The doors of the theater shove open before the rope wrenches them back. Its thick material is absorbing the abuse from their tiny hands. The knot isn't. I watch each shove extend further out in the yo-yo process from the back seat of the car. The dog pile of their shrieking faces comes into view for pulses of time.

"Alicia, we need to go." The warning in my voice pulls Alicia's head over her shoulder to see what I am watching.

"Shit." Alicia thrusts the car into reverse. The tires scream against the asphalt as if they too have seen what is trying to pursue us.

Another fling of the gears and the car lurches forward towards the Jeep that has been waiting for us at the exit. The knot has relented, allowing the children to escape from their prison. They rush into the parking lot, spilling around the cars and screaming their outrage. Like a satanic children's chorus, their wails fill the area with the different pitches of their voices.

With us safely on the streets pulling away from them, the children slow with their bodies returning to the inanimate state of saving their energy for the next chance they may find to hunt. Some part of them knows this chase is pointless. So they wait with just their eyes following us down the street from heads tilted in different degrees. Their faces go back to mute, bored expressions with time meaning nothing to them.

I have to laugh when I notice where their pursuit has halted. They stand with the backdrop of the white van spread behind them. The clowns dance, peeking from behind them, with their floating balloons casting a twisted image of a birthday party. The children have come full circle. They stand by the same method of transportation that brought them here that fateful day months ago.

"Can't hurt to look?" The question echoes in my mind. We were wrong.

The Jeep slows, coasting to a stop ahead of us when we are a few miles from the theater. Alicia pulls beside it and cuts our engine. She collapses against the steering wheel with a similar effect mimicked by the rest of us. We have had enough time to settle our hearts but our bodies are exhausted.

Dawn is breaking. The first rays of the sun are chasing away the dark night sky. Stars start to retreat, their shine diminished by the sun's glory. We were attacked twice in one night, but the sun still shines, proving that we live to see another day.

I exit the car, feeling the need to feel the sun as it breaks through the darkness. Pastel shades of orange and hues of pinks extend like fingers stretching after being a long clamped fist. The sun is the palm from which they extend and it holds the hope that we each crave to discover again. Stepping away from the car, I let myself focus on just the colors painting the sky. I let go of all the fear and despair tonight has brought me. I release the guilt I have carried. I simply stand, watching and wondering if somewhere, someone is doing the same. We have survived and no matter what comes today or the many tomorrows we still may face, it can't take that away from us.

"Pretty," Peyton stands beside me watching the colors mesh together. "It is easy to forget sometimes there are still pretty things left around us."

"Even if we are standing in blood covered clothing?" I tease him, knowing what I must look like and refusing to think he was flirting.

"Even if we are standing in blood covered clothing." He nudges me with his arm and a smile. He tells me, "You were pretty brave back there. Taking that thing on like that."

"I don't know what you two find so amusing. If tonight wasn't proof that there is no hope left for us, then I don't know what more you need to happen to see it." Alicia says, breaking into our conversation feeling defeated and broken. She tells us, "There is nowhere safe anymore. Every time we think we are, they come. They find us. I'm so tired of running."

She hangs her head, trying to hide her tears with her dark brown hair. Her arms are crossed, holding herself, so afraid to be touched because she fears it will break that last straw of strength she is fighting to tightly hold. We give her the space she needs, as my sister was never one to climb her walls willingly. She is the fighter between the two of us, but when it comes to her emotions, she is the runner.

"We will find somewhere. I have to believe that. I have to believe that there is a place where we will be safe, or what is the point to keep going? There are other people out there, just like us. Just trying to make it. We'll find them." Peyton's pep talk was meant for Alicia, but he meets everyone's eyes when he says it. He tries to share his beliefs with his conviction, stirring some sense of hope inside us, but words are not enough anymore. Filled with so much doubt, not even Terrence, with his hero worship of the man, can look at him. "We don't know if we are the only ones left from our camp. They may have chosen to go out on their own, to just keep driving. We can't know for sure. We may never know, but we can't let that deter us or break us. I'm not ready to just lie down and wait for those things to kill me. As long as I am able, I will keep fighting. I will fight for every sunrise and I will remember every person we've lost. But I will not, I cannot, believe that there is no hope. Not after how far we have come. I won't. I won't believe that." Peyton's voice started out gentle, coaxing our attention to him. It ended embedded in steel with his refusal to die.

"There has to be a place." Terrence echoes the sentiment. He pulls Kent close to him, hugging the only family he has left with the obvious desire to see to his safety. Not just his body safe, but just like me, he wants some semblance of a life for his kid.

This is no way for a sixteen-year-old to live.

"We have got to find some kind of steady place or at least more people. If anymore of us die, the kids may be left alone." Collin voices his fear. "Who is going to look after them?"

Please Lord, don't let my daughter see me die today.

"Say we do find new people, how do we know we can trust them? What safety is there really in numbers anymore? How are we going to divide up what supplies we keep finding with more people?" Alicia asks as her walls are rebuilding brick by mortar brick.

Who will be the first to scuff the lines drawn in the sand?

Genny and Kent are staring at each other. They are lost in the adult debate that is being held around them. For them, the only real question they have is centered around their growing feelings for each other.

In a weird twist of fate, the reason we came here may just become the reason that we have to stay.

My past thoughts lap around me, edging me forward with the decision that I know I must make. The way Ginjer has been staring at me with disapproval, she also knows what is about to happen.

"I may know a place." The words that I have been dreading free themselves from my tongue. Finally, I feel as if I can exhale now that the decision has been made.

"No," Ginjer comes toward me with anger trailing her. "We can't take them in. He's been bitten for God's sake."

She is pointing at Kent, but I don't understand what she is saying.

"His leg," she explains, when I don't catch on to her reason, sharing the same shock and perceptions. "Those things bit him. That's how he got the wound."

"...and I have been clawed." I am still not comprehending her fear of Kent.

"He's been bitten. He could *turn*!" Ginjer stresses the last word, drawing the one syllable out to make it more ominous than it is.

I put all the pieces together now. All of her animosity for the boy she has been expressing is all from her fear of his leg. Her fears of how the wound happened, and what she fears in her mind that it could possibly mean for the rest of us.

"Turn? What are you talking about? Turning?" Kent's voice is a high octave of outrage over what has been insinuated about him. "I'm not turning!"

"Now just wait a minute –" Terrence begins his defense of his son, but Peyton cuts him off before the conversation melts into anger and insults.

"Everyone just wait a minute. Let's all just breathe for a moment." Peyton stares at the divide that has formed with one mistrustful sentence.

Peyton looks to Ginjer, trying to diffuse the ticking bomb that she is. He says, "It doesn't seem to work like that."

"It always works like that." Ginjer is adamant in her logic.

"Lived through many things like this before?" Terrence smirks with his mocking jest. It sends Ginjer right back on the offensive.

"No, but I have never fallen asleep while people were counting on me either. Is that how he got the bite to begin with?" Ginjer's words are slow and calculated. She doesn't rush into her insult, but lets the timing propel the verbal injury.

Terrence is on his feet in an instant from where he was leaning against his Jeep. The whites of his eyes are large with his anger, but there is nothing he can do against the truth. He deflates quickly with his guilt overcoming him.

"He got the bite because we all failed. We didn't check the area well enough before we took a break in driving. We just pulled over." Collin shrugs, sharing the blame for a tragic mistake. "It's not any one person's fault, but people don't turn when bit. You either live or you die, but you don't turn."

Ginjer is shrouded in confusion. Her logic made such sense to her that now with it being proven false, she is having a hard time letting it go.

"Lady, I don't mean to upset you, but with all you have seen in just these two days, you mean to tell me the fact that people don't turn is what is confusing to you the most?" Collin smiles at her with honest sincerity. There is no mocking in his voice. Ginjer has to relent with nothing more to add to her fire. I wonder what kind of wife Collin used to have to be able to handle my sister and someone as high maintenance as Ginjer so easily.

"What do you mean you may know a place?" Collin attempts to work his same soothing balm upon me.

With Ginjer reluctantly staring at me and Genny pleading with me, I start the conversation that I have been fearing for so long. I tell them everything. I tell them why we were at the store that day. I explain to them my reasons for not speaking up sooner. I tell them about the graveyard and the rows of crypts just waiting for as many people as we discover. I outline the logic of it. I explain how it has kept us safe for so long. I talk as the sun rises fully into the sky behind me. I explain it all like a confessor to a priest because at the end of my speech, I ask for their forgiveness for not sharing sooner for the deaths it might have prevented if I had.

In the end, and after many answered questions, they understand. As Collin points out with his customary charm, why would I trust people that attempted to kidnap us. Genny is a ball of joy that she will not have to be separated from Kent. The teens' reaction makes Terrence and I both smirk at each other. He jokingly calls me "Mom" under his breath as we spread the map out on the hood of my car. For some reason, he finds it all way more amusing than I do.

We plot the path back to the place I have become accustomed to calling home. It feels as if I have been on a long journey and my mind craves the comfort of my own bed. A bed that is lodged behind rows of sealed caskets. A home that belongs to the dead, but they share well enough.

"It's really going to be alright?" Alicia's voice is filled with wonder over the prospect as I drive behind the Jeep.

The tone makes Genny and I smile. It pulls a smirk from the still tense Ginjer, even.

"It might be nice to have some men around." There is Ginjer, always one for a positive aspect. Make a silver lining a chance for her to be the center of male attention and she will find it. Bless her heart.

Chapter 16

It has been a few months since that night at the theater. It took some adjusting for them, at first, to be comfortable with the concept of "crypt living" as Kent dubbed it. With the men's help, we were able to move the remaining caskets completely. Our conscience got the best of us though so we buried them in the grounds behind our row, still keeping them close to their original resting places. It seemed to help our guilt over the matter and it gave us fuel to tease the kids. Every time they hear a sound, we tell them it is the ghost of those we removed looking for their bodies. The kids are not as amused by this as we are.

Collin and Alicia moved into their own "home". She confesses to me that sometimes she feels wrong finding her happiness only because of the death of his family. To which I always ask her if staying miserable is a better alternative. It seems to calm her soul a little, but she still flashes me a nervous smile when they hold hands around us. I want them to be happy. After everything we have endured, we all deserve to be happy.

Ginjer remains aloof. She partakes in the new camaraderie, but never really lets anyone close. Being back here undoubtedly reminds of her Mintzy and I feel sorry for her. She never said a word as Terrence buried the dog's remains when we arrived, but Genny made a little grave marker just the same. Ginjer will ask me questions sometimes about the children at the theater before she falls silent again.

I think the sight of them made all of this more real for her. The first week we were home, Ginjer often asked to stay in my crypt even if it was an "utter mess of disorganization".

My wounds from that night were not as deep as they appeared. Ginjer was able to perform another "surgery" and they healed just fine. I have my first "battle scars" as Peyton calls the half-moons on my arms and the small lines on my neck.

Peyton and I have grown close. We are not as close as Genny hints with her lewd tones and late night giggling, but close. I think sometimes she worries for me, but with how much risk life involves now, I just don't know if I can find the courage to open another room in my heart for someone.

He chose to room with Terrence and Kent calling their "crypt living" the frat house. With the loud male laughter that can be heard from it during the day, I find it fitting. Since at the root of most of the antics around here is them, it is very fitting.

I had forgotten what it was like to have a "family". Our days went from hiding and sneaking around to hanging out with others in a crypt chosen for just that purpose. Inside it, we have our supplies and even slight decorations we scavenged from runs. We have lawn chairs and Kent put a box resembling a T.V. that the store used to display furniture settings. "Toss me the remote," joke is heard often and even after all this time it can still bring a smile.

We have settled into routines and roles as life goes on. We are shadows of our past lives. We pull from that existence the strengths and knowledge that we developed adding to this world while we are discovering parts of us that we may have never known existed before. We are just remnants now of who we once were, trying to form a new whole.

We haven't had any run-ins with the monsters in weeks, leaving some of us hopeful it may be coming to an end. We haven't seen any people either, though. If it is coming to an end, I only wonder how many are left.

Christmas has come and gone. Nights are reaching freezing temperatures finally as winter roars with her presence. Frost often coats the ground making the place sparkle under the early morning sun. Kent discovered that a cardboard box slides well over the frozen grass and he is often out there first thing slipping around. I have a feeling that Ginjer will be putting more stitches in his leg soon.

On one supply run, Terrence came across a piece of paper left on a store counter. It read that there was a shelter set up at a high school further upstate. It has supplies and medical aid for those that need them. Once again, we found our "hope".

As I write this, we have been driving for hours and are getting ready to take a break. The men are preparing the last of our supplies. Peyton and Collin had figured out how much food and such we would need to make this trip. We left the rest behind in case we needed to return. If it does prove to be false, it is not as if the "crypt living" is going anywhere. We can always return and settle back into this life, but if it is true, we can't pass up the chance to explore the possibility.

"I can't believe you brought those." Genny leans against the car, staring at me with a mildly amused face.

"If we stay, I wanted to be sure to have them. They hold more than just my ramblings." I smile at her, pulling out a small Ziploc bag from between the back pages.

"I stand corrected. Now I can't believe you." Her voice is a combination of shock and happiness staring at the clear bag in my hand and her grinning first grade face that stares up at her.

"I couldn't not grab some. Obviously, I couldn't fit all of the scrap books in the bags but I wanted to have something." I spread out the pictures of years slipped past on the back seat of the car. I watch as Genny goes from joyful innocence to awkward middle school to the young woman she is now in a collection of small portraits.

"Is that Dad?" Genny picks the photo up of her and her father fishing from the pier of a local beach. The fish she had hooked was bigger than her, bending the pole with its weight. She cried when he told her that it would die if she tried to keep it as a pet. She just couldn't understand why it would not like to live with her in the bathtub. So began her year long mermaid obsession she developed.

Genny takes her own journey down her memory lane, touching the photos as if they are ancient holy relics. To me, they are. It's all I have left of what she was.

"Oh jeez, Mom," She holds up a "Happy Mother's Day" she made in kindergarten.

"Really?" She asks me and I playfully snatch it from her.

"Don't tease me. This was my very first Mother's Day card. This thing lived at the bottom of my purse for a long time." I stare at the construction paper card with a yearning for a time long gone.

The pastel purple paper has a crudely cut out heart of pink felt glued to the center of it. White lace was glued around the heart framing it with misguided precision. In some spots, the gold glitter that stuck to everything the card touched still remains. Scrawled around the heart are the words "Happy Mofers Day". What Genny groans over today in shame still touches my heart with the adoration only a parent can understand.

Staring back at me from inside the card is a wide-grinning Genny, with her front tooth missing, from a miniature photo her teacher had taken in class just for this project. The same segmented scrawl fills the space under the photo. "I Luv U! Genny" All around it are glue stains showing where glitter once clung to the paper. Two days after receiving this card, Charlie had asked for a divorce. I carried the card with me everywhere to help me through the dark days of depression. It seemed only right to grab it as I was throwing things in the bags when we left our home.

"What do you think happened here?" she asks me, while we place the tender relics back into their bag. All except the card. With an eye roll from my daughter, I place that one in the pocket of my blue jeans over-come with the need to have it close to me.

I stare out into the lot of the Welcome Center where we have stopped. Plywood has been removed from the door sections, allowing the entrance to be exposed. Bones are scattered through a section in front of what was once the gift shop/diner combination parking lot. With the passage of seasons, it is still easy to tell that the streaks on the broken glass doors are not just dirt, but something more sinister. Peyton reported that the building itself had been ransacked long ago with the elements of nature spread wide within. Whatever happened here, happened long ago. We are just looking at the residual haunting of it.

"Dunno," I tell her. "But whatever it was, it was long ago. There is nothing here now. That is the few good things about snow. No footprints. No baddies."

I earn another eye roll but it comes with a smile as well. I'll take it.

"Hey," Alicia is waving her arms, slipping her way towards us on the frozen ground.

"Five dollars says she busts her ass." Genny arches an eyebrow with her dare.

"Really?" I mockingly smack her arm. "You should know better than to talk like that. Besides, we know she is going to bust her ass."

Karma picks just that moment to bring my older sister down, flat on her ass.

"Don't let her see you laugh." I warn Genny with her giggle-snickering coughs. We make our treacherous way to Alicia with none of us accustomed to the "black ice" as Peyton calls it.

"Did you just want to be sure we saw you fall or did you have a reason for calling to us?" It is not often I get the chance to tease my sister. I'm not missing the chance now.

"Totally give you a 7.8 for the dismount from walking. I would have given you a nine, but the arm work as you came down looked a little sloppy." Genny claps with her jest, growing brave from my remark.

Real funny. Now help me up." Alicia extends her hands out to us, cranky and sore. Her eyes are still the normal shades of her green-teal so we are safe from her wrath, for now.

Once she is on her feet again, shaky at best, she tells us about the showers they have found inside the store. The back of the place served as a truck stop. The water no longer runs, but there is enough in our supplies to be at least able to rinse off. Peyton has begun bottling the snow to boil for later uses if we run low. We won't be shaving our legs anytime soon, but at least we will have clean hair. It's the small things in life that can really make a girl smile.

The diner exits into a long windowless hallway. Normally rows of rectangular, fluorescent lights would guide the way from the ceiling, but we have to use flashlights. The beams dance across the dirty, greying floor and the walls with the circular light chasing away the fears of the dark. It is not that we fear the dark. We fear what lives in the dark. Monsters come in many forms and they are often never standing under the sun waving with ample warning that they are near.

Tall lockers with mesh, metal doors provide clues that we are nearing the shower area. They alternate in colors of red, white, and blue with the strategic hopes of adding more proof of how Americanly wholesome this place once was for customers. The same theme continues with the shower room doors across the hall from each other. Their red paint stands bold against the white walls of the hallway. Matching the blue paint from the lockers are words explaining which side is to be used by which sex.

"Let's use the "Men's"." Genny smiles at me. The simple rules of life no longer matter, but it is still fun to break them with mischievous innocence.

"Do we know where the guys are?" I look to Alicia for my answer before giving Genny hers. That would be "parent of the year" to agree only to walk right into a bunch of showering nude males.

"Ginjer is showing them how to break into the trucks that are parked in the back. Kent seems to think he can wire the CB radios with the solar panels we found so that we can have "phone service" in the crypts. I think the guys just wanted to see what supplies they could find. I swear though, if they think we are going to ride around in one of those things, they are crazy. Gas is hard enough to find as it is for our cars." Alicia tells us, pressing her palms against the swinging door to open it.

"He's such a geek." Genny mutters, following her aunt into the bathroom, but her smile shows a smidge of pride. Then again, she is a teen. She may just be happy about the thought of having a "phone".

The interior of the shower room is the same Americana pride style of décor. The once white tiles and walls stand barren with more bright red lockers attached to them. In front of the lockers are benches painted in a proud blue. Words upon the wall match the color, declaring freedom from grime in a coy play on words. The simple paint job must have not cut much into the overhead of this place.

Long, sideways, narrow windows along the outside wall allows light into the room making the flashlights finally unnecessary. There is little to no destruction to this room. It is a stark comparison to the rest of the building with the amount of debris scattered throughout the diner and store from past mayhem that has occurred.

Only the lockers show signs of abuse. Their doors stand at various degrees of being opened, with pieces of the broken locks on the floor. Damaged gym bags sit empty among the metal fragments with their cavities searched and their contents spilled around them. Compared to the other places we have explored, this place feels homey.

Towels from our stash are waiting for us along the rim of the metal sinks. Genny is disappointed that her plans for breaking the rules were side-stepped by the plans already put into place. She gives me a mock frown before snatching a waiting towel and heading to a stall.

"We thought it would be safer to use the same room. They guys already have made sure the door to the other is secured so we don't have any more surprises like the theater." Alicia offers the logic of the plan with hopes to appease the pouting teen. Unfortunately, when a teen starts to pout, there is no appeasing the beast that they become. Well executed ignorance of the mood swing is always best.

"Whatever," Genny mutters. She is more overcome with disappointment for feeling silly over her excitement to be in the "Men's" room than she is with her aunt.

I shake my head letting Alicia know to drop it.

The men have already placed the large gallon jugs that hold our water in each stall. Soap stains streak down the tiled wall from the dispensers of shampoo and conditioner further proving that this is a male locker room. I am willing to bet the female's room is empty of all spare soap. Just another example of how differently our minds work.

Living in close circumstances removes some social phobias but not all. We each enter into our own stalls and pull the vinyl curtains closed with a metallic ringing sound. Our clothes neatly fold and slide into the far corner of the stall with the towel. Because of the shyness over our nudity, conversation isn't started again until after the first shrieks from pouring the cold water over our heads. I turn a deaf ear to the words Genny screams, but laugh just the same over hearing her degree of expletives.

The water is biting cold on my scalp. Its iciness feels to reach my brain and leave a dull headache with its exit. The shampoo is a boring male scent of basic soap. I am thankful there are no clouds of steam to carry the fragrance through the room with its sharp soap smell. The conditioner is void of any perfumes or undertones but I am happy to have clean hair just the same. Still heavy from the water, but I can already feel a difference to the feel of it.

We dress much as we undressed. The only difference is the shyness is gone. After hearing your daughter drop more words than you personally know, a little thing like nudity behind a shower curtain seems unimportant.

"Does Kent know you talk like that?" Alicia teases her as we stand at the rows of mirrors on the little divider wall separating the locker area and shower area.

Now that we are fully dressed, we enjoy the bonding time this presents with just the three of us. Amid our laughter, we brush our hair and try to remove as much excess water as we can with the limp towels before having to go back into the winter wind.

"Who do you think taught me them?" Genny strikes an exaggerated sultry pose in the mirror.

We laugh watching her, knowing fully well the saint that she is.

"What else has he taught you?" Alicia snaps the wet towel at Genny, causing her to shriek with the impact.

"Alicia Helen Clark," I call to my sister with a look of teasing disagreement. "Virgins live to the end. You just keep remembering that, Genny!"

"Guess that means you two are screwed." Once again, my daughter shocks me with her wit. My mouth hangs open with surprise and amusement.

"Nah, it's been so long for your mom she may count as a virgin again." They both laugh staring at me, waiting for some kind of verbal defense. Unfortunately, I have none.

"Cute. Real cute." My response only brings more laughter from them.

The walls echo with the sounds from it and even if the target of their teasing is me, my laughter soon echoes as well.

Our conversation has calmed with the topic of what we each hope to find at the high school. Genny wants to find more people of her age, or at least close. We tease her about boys and about what poor Kent will do if there are any. Alicia hopes to learn what exactly all of this is about or at least some plan to survive it. When they look at me, I don't know what to say. In my pause a tapping sound comes from the other room; a light drumming of finger tips perhaps on the metal outside door. We smile thinking it is one of the guys checking on us, but being shy about it, fearing what he may see if he just walks in.

When the hinges creak with the slow, steady opening of the door, Alicia winks at us. She walks around her corner of the small divider wall plotting to surprise someone, but when she runs back and pulls us to the floor, her wide eyes and shaking hands tell us it is we who are about to receive a surprise.

Chapter 17

Alicia holds a quivering finger to her full, pursed lips telling us not to ask any questions. There is only one thing left to this world that makes someone shake this hard. We don't need to ask anything at all.

With our backs pressed to the mirrors, we listen to the shuffling feet sliding along the tiles in the adjoining room. It whispers to us, warning us of the path they are taking. The locker doors clang with their metallic hints as the monsters draw closer to our side of the room. With a serial killer's torment, each door rings out with its slamming audibly torturing us with each sound that grows closer. We jump with each loud clang, creeping further to the opposite corner of the wall to escape the noise. When the noise stops, the pounding of my heart fills the white noise of my panic.

The sounds stopped short of the wall, giving us no further proof of a path of travel or hints of progression. The whispering shuffles have evaporated. However many there are, they are either standing still or are waiting right behind the wall we are now hiding behind. A thousand pictures of what they are doing and how many are waiting for us parade through my mind.

Genny has her hands clamped over her mouth to prevent the sounds of her sobbing from reaching them. I squeeze her other hand, trying to lend her the strength I am pretending to contain.

Alicia lays flat on the cold tiles. She shimmies along the floor until she can see around the corner before pulling back to us. Sitting back up with her back against the mirror, she stares at the vacant stalls across from us. Her jaw muscles flex with her somber thoughts. I know from her reaction that we are outnumbered and our escape is blocked. We have no way to call for help. If we are going to get out of here, it is up to us to think of something, and fast.

My sister and I share a look over Genny's quaking body. The determination we share with it rebuilds our bravery layer by shared layer. This is all that is left of our family, sitting here pinned, and we both silently agree that we are not willing to lose each other again.

"Make a noise to draw them to the other corner," I offer a plan with a breath barely above a whisper. "Maybe it will bring them to that side and we can crawl behind them to the door."

"There are too many." Alicia shakes her head, rejecting it.

"How many?" Genny asks, fearing the answer but afraid to not know, too.

"I counted seven," Alicia says, "but I can't be sure."

Genny has started to shut down her emotions. She is swallowing against the fear with hopes to clear her head. She says, "Mom's idea is the only way then."

My sister looks at me again. I arch one eyebrow asking if she can think of anything before our time runs out. Her eyes roll and sigh tells me she can't.

"You ready?" I ask them, but I am also asking myself. Once this starts to play out, there is no detour to the ending, whatever it may end up being.

They nod and we slide as close as we can to the corner that sits near the wall where the door waits. It should be a simple plan. We will draw their attention to the other side and when we see them start to come in, we will slip around the divider wall, staying low to the ground, and crawl to the door. As long as there are no more in the hallway, we will be able to escape to the parking lot where the rest of the group waits. It sounds simple enough in my head, but plans always do.

I crawl to the sink, staying as close to the wall as I can in case something comes around the corner before I am ready to run. I try to block out the thoughts of what we are about to do as my fingers fumble for the brush's handle that projects from the rim of the sink. It scrapes along the metal as I pull it down to me and it is as loud as a banshee's wail in so much forced silence. If there were any second thoughts, my folly has stolen that option. The first shuffle heads our way.

The screeching came from the middle sink where we were standing moments ago. The noise not being on any definite side could bring them around both corners. If that happens, they will block us and we will have no way out. My clumsiness may have just killed us.

My stomach is a sour pit of dread as I crawl back to them. Alicia's eyes are closed with her head resting back against the mirror while we wait to see what happens now. We are inmates sitting on death row with all the anxiety and prayers that it brings.

Please Lord, don't let my daughter see me die today.

Footsteps, more eager now than the whispering shuffling of before with the proof that something is in here, come our way. The locker doors start slamming again, louder this time in the rush to reach the sound they heard. Their excitement causes them to make short, guttural vocal sounds. It jars my fears, speeding my pulse to hear so many of them so close.

Genny sobs again, no longer needing to hide the sound. She is shaking so hard that my arm trembles with the force from it. I squeeze her hand, pulling her wild eyes towards me.

"Get ready," I whisper to her. My voice is barely heard over the many excited noises from the other side of the wall that make their way to us.

We will have to move quickly to avoid being seen. They are searching for something now, where as before, they were exploring due to the sounds of our laughter. Their hunting skills are fully awake. They are hunting for us.

When the first leg comes around the other corner, Alicia leads us around our corner. I pray the row of sinks will block us from their sight, allowing us the time to slip away. We press our backs to the back of the wall we just left, and wait for as many as we can to go around, removing them from this space. Monsters don't play by plans and we hit the first mistake of ours.

Finding nothing on that side of the wall, the first few slip back into an exploring mode. They slow down from the rushing pace they set and block the last few from turning the corner. Standing even with us, we stare at them afraid to even breathe.

The woman who is the closest to us is barely wearing her once fitted suit. Her body has become sunken-in hollows and jutting joints. She is barefoot, exposing the bones of her feet from the layers of damage the snow and ice have done to them. Her skirt hangs low on her hips with the wide, elastic band no longer needed to help hold it where a large belly once stretched it holding the new life within her safe. Her thighs are caked with the blood from her miscarriage. She was pregnant when she became what she is now and her body expelled the life that was inside her, staining her flesh with its departure.

Next to her is another woman that was not as well-dressed when her life ended. Her basic blue jeans are discolored in various patterns at various spots. There is mud and dirt adhered to her calves as if she waded through something at one time. Her tennis shoes are a ruin from the dragging and the weather. Her basic grey tee shirt has fared no better. Its cotton collar is stretched and hangs loosely around her neck. The flesh of one arm is gone. It's a weaving of tendons and muscles with congealed thick, black blood that splatters to the white tiles. The blood no longer flows through her veins. It is only as useful as oil is to a car, keeping the moving parts lubed and moving. It falls from her just as dark and thick.

The scent of their decaying bodies surrounds us, giving a weight to the air as if I could taste it on my tongue. We are panting with fear and the attempts to overcome the smell of their putrid decomposition. We might as well be trying to inhale acid with how it burns our lungs. My stomach rolls with it, bringing tart bile to my tongue.

They will turn soon and see us. The first few may come around my corner any moment, encircling us. We are waiting, letting precious seconds be stolen from us with the terror that holds us imprisoned, unable to move or breathe. Unless one of us moves, the spell will not be broken.

Please Lord, don't let my daughter see me die today.

Pitching my body slowly forward, I start to crawl through the room that grows in length before me. I spare a quick glance over my shoulder, hoping that Genny will follow me. I hope her fear of being left alone will carry her forward unlike her fear of the monsters that keep her a prisoner. I crawl on my knees and forearms, doing my best to keep low to the ground. Genny follows my example, scrambling after me and leaving Alicia to follow.

We pass bench after bench as they are searching the stalls. The metal rings protest the sharp sliding along the metal poles of the showers. I can hear the vinyl curtains as they are shoved aside or being completely ripped apart. The howls of their anger are growing with each empty stall that they discover. With the red door looming before me, I can almost touch our salvation with my fingers.

"Elizabeth!" Flipping my head around to see behind me with my name screamed from my sister, I see that our time has run out. The woman in what's left of the suit is heading right for us.

With no reason left to crawl, I stand, pulling Genny up with me, and force her to run the last few inches to the door. Alicia's scream has brought all of them around the wall. A collection of decrepit bodies enrage at our sight, screaming out in a battle cry from Hell for our deaths. The freezing weather has done its destruction to their exposed bodies. It adds extra monstrosities to the creatures that chase us. Being starved for so long fuels them with intense rage and eagerness to destroy everything they can. Right now, it's us that they want to feed from. Their mouths crave our bodies to taste. It's our flesh for which their fingers hook with hopes of raking chunks from, spilling the hot blood that is the nectar of life for them. A room that seemed so long when we were crawling now shrinks rapidly as they run towards us.

I continue to shove Genny forward with Alicia holding onto my hand. Touching one another, we keep our bond and refuse to be separated, but it slows us, making us clumsy. Genny slips on the black ooze-like substance one of them has left behind, smearing the drops into a long streak on the tiled floor. Refusing to place her behind me, I stop to steady her shaking body and we lose the fragment of the space we held between them.

The suited woman lunges for Alicia, jerking her backwards and my arm with her. My sister's screams puncture my sanity and I'm paralyzed watching them attack her. Their hands rip through her clothing, pulling red, dripping pieces from her body like a summer's ripe watermelon. Mouths gnaw at her neck, lacerating her veins. Her blood pumps and pours from the wounds, arching outwards, showering her with her death. The tiles at her feet become pools of crimsons and bright reds. It spreads from her like jars of broken jam. The smallest of them drops to those tiles, licking and sucking the floor. He rubs his face into it as if he were a cat, stroking his fur.

I am locked and deaf to my surroundings. I can only see my sister being destroyed so ferociously that their acts support her still standing body when her knees fall out from under her. Her mouth is open with her screams, but I can't hear her. She stares at me, but the light is fading from her teal-green eyes. We still clutch each other's hand, but I can feel her grasp growing weaker.

I want to hold on to her, disproving what I am seeing, refusing to let her go now that I have found her. Genny is screaming my name. The sounds travel down a long tunnel, expanding the syllables. Alicia's fingers slide from my hand when she falls to the ground like a broken angel. All that keeps me from following her down is my daughter's screams. With a "pop", time catches up to me as my sister fades from view amid a disarray of carnage and growling forms. One shaky step at a time, I walk backwards to my name and shut the door behind me. My older sister, Alicia Helen Clark, is dead.

"We have to go!" Genny is pulling on me to move.

I can already hear their screams starting from the other side of the door. They have already destroyed Alicia and are hungry for more. There will be no running from them, not now. You can't outrun death.

Images of Alicia and myself at different times of our lives play like a silent movie in my mind. Memories of us flow past like a silent slide show of heart-touching moments. I watch us running by the beach, chasing the waves that we were both too small and too scared to swim. I watched her soar past me on the swings, her brown hair flowing in the wind behind her as she launches into the air, always being the brave one. Our laughter at "borrowing" our parent's car for late night food runs when they are asleep. Weddings, separations, laughter, tears, it all flashes before me like an invitation to which I have already sent my RSVP. Hands test the door that I am pushing. There will be no running today.

"Mom!" Genny is screaming for me as she side-steps down the hallway. Something on my face slows her.

"What is the plan?" My voice is hoarse and my eyes sting with unshed tears.

"No. No, we can do this. Mom, please…" Her tears spill forth with the same flurry as her words.

"What is the plan?" I ask her again, this time with more conviction. Fingertips tap on the door behind me.

"Get out. My safety first, only then help others. Think with your head, not your heart." Her voice cracks with each word. The sentences are paused with her unsteady breathing.

"The notebooks?" I prod her, helping her to focus and remember. Nails claw at the paint, unable to fully press the door open yet with my weight blocking them.

"Use the notebooks to figure out what stores have been looted and which ones have not. Keep track of where people have set up to avoid them. Use the side roads. Never the main ones." She recites the words we have practiced knowing that this time it is not just a rehearsal.

"You'll be fine. You'll be brave. Keep close to Peyton. Find that high school and you live. You survive this." The first real push comes and I stumble before reapplying pressure.

"You can't leave me! I can't do this alone…" She has already begun to take small steps backwards, still praying I will join her. Her face begs me to run with her, attempting to call my bluff, but I'm not bluffing. There are too many of them for us to both run and survive. I can buy my daughter the time she needs to make it.

The door bounces again, and I know this is what I have to do, because the truth is, I can't do it without *her.*

"Yes, you can. Listen to me." I talk over her moan of refusal. "Listen! Nothing is how it used to be. I don't know if it ever will be again. You will have to do things now that you don't want to do. Some things will rip your heart right out, Genny girl. It won't make you a bad person. It just makes you a survivor. You remember that," I tell her, fighting against the door. As their eagerness grows, so does their strength. "Not all choices are easy anymore, but we have to make them. Just like what you are going to do now. You are going to run. Stick to the plan. You have to survive. You have to survive for me and for your aunt. You have to keep going to wherever this takes you. Don't you ever give up, Genny. Don't you ever give up on life."

Each sobbing step leads her further away from me. I fight back my tears. Her last sight of me will not be of me sobbing and scared, but of a strong woman that believes in her. I know this moment will haunt her, but she won't be haunted by my weakness. She'll be haunted by my love.

The door presses harder against my back, thumping me with a sudden shove.

"Go, Genny. Go! I love you. Now run. Run, Genny girl! You run!" I shout at her, commanding her to move before it's too late. Genny breaks down in sorrow, but my voice finally reaches her and she turns from me to run.

She runs from the sight of what is inevitable. She runs from her shame of living another day while I stay behind. She runs from the pain of losing her family. She runs. My little girl runs away.

I slide down to the floor, wedging my knees up to provide better traction to fight against their strength and the desperation to be free from that room. Their savage nature that craves our flesh forces them to beat against the metal with no concern for themselves.

A piece of paper crinkles in my pocket and reminds me of the treasure I hold. Pulling out the purple and pink card, I open it to stare at her smiling face. Genny's grinning face of innocence with the joys of wonder that each day brought to her at that age smiles up at me. I am reminded of Becky and

I wonder if somewhere a mother is staring at a similar photo of a little girl that never was able to grow up. A little girl who was never returned to her.

Happy Mofers Day", it tells me. Today is my Mother's Day. Today is the day I do what all mothers know they would do for their children. Happy Mofers Day.

Staring at the paper, I remember an inscription of a blood-baptized angel with sad pale eyes and crumbling stone wings.

Stand not before me and weep. Let not your wails of mourning fill the air around me. For from this life's suffering I am free. Soon, all will join me and we will rejoice in our victory.

Clutching the card to my chest, I stand, stepping away from the door and letting what will be, will be.

Please Lord, don't let my daughter see me die today.

Chapter 18

I explode through the door, almost falling from the ice on the cement. Mr. Peyton is standing by our car with the rest of the group. Mrs. Ginjer stands when seeing me and she knows that something is wrong. She knows that three went in, but only I am coming out. Her fear-filled posture turns the rest towards me with slow, hesitant movements.

I refuse to think of my mother waiting in the hallway or thoughts of my aunt dead in the locker room. I try to block out the picture of them attacking, killing the women that I have known as my rock, while I run away like a coward. My feet slip, almost gliding towards the group with my haste.

"We have to go. Now!" I don't stop to explain anything more. The words will destroy me if I have to speak them out loud.

Mr. Peyton slides in the driver's seat of our car not asking for any explanations. Mrs. Ginjer runs to the passenger side, leaving me in the back seat. Mr. Collin opens the door for me, helping me inside. I can't meet his questioning eyes. I just can't.

Mr. Terrence hurriedly pulls himself behind the wheel of the Jeep and Kent rushes to get in on the other side. Their southern Jeep pulls around our compact, letting their larger tires make a path in the snow and ice for us to follow. Kent is pressed up against his window as they pass. My eyes lock with his and their many questions place a crack in the resolve I was fighting to hold.

My mother's notebook sits on the floor in front of me. Picking it up, I run my fingers over the worn cardboard. I flip through the pages of her script where she has left all of her secret thoughts and fears from that which she protected me. I remember going through the Ziploc bag just hours ago with the many versions of myself that stare back at me. There are no pictures of my mother or aunt in this bag. My resolve is gone and I let forth the pain that I tried to deny.

Soft sobs turn into wails that shock me. My chest feels as if it is bursting and breaking at the same time from the pain of their deaths. I can't pull in enough air to keep up with my misery. I am alone. My family is gone. I left them behind to die so that I may escape.

Mr. Collin pulls me to him and rocks me. I hear his whispered words through his chest. Their soothing rumble contradicts with the fast beating of his heart. He is fighting his own misery over losing my aunt.

"I don't think we have ever been properly introduced," he tells me, whispering the words into my dark brown hair so much like my aunt's. "My name is Collin Hawthorn. Your aunt and I had a daughter together twenty-four years ago. That makes you my niece in a way, too."

He pulls my face from his chest with gentle hands, holding my face so that I am looking straight into his blue, blue eyes that are spilling forth as many tears as mine.

"So, you see, we are family. You and I. You're not all alone now and neither am I," he tells me, reading the thoughts of my drowning soul.

I hug him, clinging to him like a port in a turbulent storm. Almost a year ago, I stayed home, avoiding a vaccine shot that brought the world to its knees with its domino effect of destruction. My mother and I ran from the monsters with Mrs. Ginjer, fighting to stay alive. Fate brought us to this group and to my aunt. We learned to trust again through them and through us they learned to live. Fate brought us to this Welcome Center that hinted at past hardships, but we didn't take heed of its warnings. We ignored the whispers left in the bones strewn across the parking lot and the mayhem inside. Now my mother and aunt are two more victims it has claimed with a chain of misery that was started long ago. I will tell everyone that asks that my mother died for me. She died so that I may live.

Once upon a time, there was a perfect girl, with a perfect life, in a perfect world. Once upon a time, that was me. Someone threw it all away for love; the love they held for me. Now I am shattered, rebuilding my heart and soul with the promised hopes of what a high school scrawled on a long forgotten note may hold. I am a remnant of the girl I once was, the life I once had. We are all remnants now, stalked by the ghosts of those we loved, just trying to form a new whole.

About the Author

Marie F Crow weaves her stories around the human element of the horror verses the 'monsters' themselves. She believes that the real horror of life does not come from the expected, but from the unexpected responses of the human nature and what depths of trauma a person must survive in certain situations. She began writing The Risen series when feeling that the popular genre was slipping too deep into the realm of pure 'slasher' and forgetting what the horror of zombies can mean for a story.

Now, with her children's series launched, Marie hopes to use her favorite 'monster' as a teaching tool to inspire children to understand that not everything that looks scary, is scary. With Abigail and Her

Pet Zombie series, Marie hopes to further spread her love for all things "that go bump in the night" with small children showing them that it's okay to be different and to embrace those same differences in those around them.

Social Media Links
Facebook: @MarieFCrow.Author
Instagram: @authormariefcrow
Twitter: @MarieFCrow

Additional titles by Marie F Crow:

The Risen Series
Dawning
Margaret
Remnants
Courage (Coming Soon)
Defiance (Coming Soon)

The Siren Series
Crown of Betrayal

The Abigail and her Pet Zombie Series
Abigail and her Pet Zombie
Zoo Day
Spring
Summer
Halloween

About the Publisher

Kingston Publishing offers an affordable way for you to turn your dream into a reality. We offer every service you will ever need to take an idea and publish a story. We are here to help authors make it in the industry. We've been hurt by publishers in the past and we want to provide a positive experience that will keep you coming back to us.

Whether you want a traditional publisher who offers all the amenities a publishing company should or an author who prefers to self-publish, but needs additional help - we are here for you.

Now Accepting Manuscripts!

Please send query letter and manuscript to:

submissions@kingstonpublishing.com

Visit our website at www.kingstonpublishing.com